DEATH BY MARRIAGE

(BOOK #3 IN THE CARIBBEAN MURDER SERIES)

JADEN SKYE

ISBN: 978-1-64029-241-3

PROLOGUE

He lay there alone, along the back alley of a narrow street that wound through the marketplace in St. Thomas, dipped in a pool of red blood. For a long while, no one noticed. The street he lay on was not well traveled, and the few people who passed through it walked around him.

As the sun rose, bringing the heat of the day, merchants began opening their shops, and shoppers taking their first tentative steps. Suddenly, a shriek broke through the quiet. The shriek sounded fiercely, like the call of a bugle, for a long, long time.

People came running. An island woman, walking through the alley, had stepped on the man. Hands over her eyes, she could not stop shrieking. The dead man's bulging eyes stared back out at her, only adding to her terror.

"Why me? Why did I have to find this? Lord, Lord!" she screamed. "Have mercy! Mercy!"

The crowd closed in, peering.

"Who is it? Who is it?" they demanded.

But by now his face was so distorted, it was almost impossible to say.

CHAPTER 1

Cindy and Mattheus sat on the veranda of the Grande Hotel in Grenada, under the palm trees, going over details of the case. They sipped tall lemonades as the afternoon light faded and soft ocean breezes drifted over them. It had been a long, tiring day. Cindy knew she would have to make a decision quickly, and had grappled with it all afternoon.

Things were moving too quickly, though. She felt caught in a whirlwind that didn't give her any time to catch her breath, to make wise choices. She had to remind herself that she'd only come down to the island to help Dalia, an old friend who'd frantically called for help. Dalia's husband had gone missing and she was devastated, and there had been no way Cindy could say no.

It had been a couple of months since then, an intense, crazy time, which only became more so when Dalia's husband turned up dead on the beach. When Cindy was the one to finally discover the killer, she had been all over the papers again. Cindy didn't want the notoriety. But calls came in for her from all over.

Mattheus tilted his head back, tapping his fingers on the table. It was something he did when he was trying to think things out clearly, Cindy had come to learn. He'd gathered lots of information on the new case, but he'd been half an hour late to their meeting, something unusual for him. Cindy had waited for him uneasily, going over everything that had gone on between them since they'd met about two months ago.

She had tentatively agreed to form a private detective agency with him. It was at a moment when she'd felt a particular connection with both him and the work. But what did she really know about him? she now wondered. He was on the police force when they'd met and he'd been a wonderful help in her friend's case. But people on this island got too close too quickly, and no good ever seemed to come out of it.

Cindy took a long, deep breath. She had both looked forward to seeing Mattheus this afternoon and also felt unnerved about it. Partially, she just wanted to run away, go back to life as she knew it in New York, before her own husband, Clint, had been killed. It had only been months since Clint was gone. She felt odd now spending such intense time with another man.

"I know you can do a great job with this case," Mattheus continued, his voice full of conviction.

"Mattheus," Cindy interrupted.

He stopped tapping his fingers and looked straight at her, his beautiful, clear eyes quieting her racing mind.

"It's natural to be scared," he said.

"That's not it," Cindy replied.

Surprisingly, Cindy did not feel scared of tackling another murder. Actually, she felt invincible at the thought of taking another case on. It was that feeling of power and service that drew her to the work. It made her feel more of who she really was.

"What is it?" Mattheus asked, a small smile curling at the edges of his mouth.

"It's a huge choice to start an entirely different life," she said.

"Yes, it is," he answered calmly, "but sometimes a new life chooses us. And you're not the only one. It will be a new life for me, too."

He looked up at her fleetingly, then looked away.

"I've gathered articles and reports about the case. It's fascinating," he continued, switching focus. "Kendra, the wife, called after reading about you in the paper. She sounded desperate. Said she wants a woman detective on the scene, someone who'll understand her point of view."

Cindy perked up.

"There aren't too many of them down here on the islands." Mattheus cocked his head to the side. "Especially as thoughtful and as smart as you."

Cindy smiled.

"And daring," he added, "and beautiful."

Despite herself Cindy laughed. "You're buttering me up."

"I'm speaking the truth. I've been thinking about our new company."

"I wasn't even sure we meant it," Cindy said hesitantly.

At that Mattheus leaned forward.

"I meant it," he said, with no hesitation. "I mean what I say." He looked at her searchingly. "How about you?"

"You've been a police officer for years," said Cindy. "I have no training."

"You have an instinctive gift. You're unstoppable. Let's go over the details of this new case before I say any more." He pulled out a file. "This woman's husband, a well-known criminal attorney in St. Thomas, the father of a daughter. He was murdered and thrown like garbage into an alleyway behind the open markets."

"Horrible," said Cindy.

"The police are focusing in on the wife. She's terrified. Not only by the loss of her husband, but by being interrogated night and day. Her entire world has been ripped apart. You can imagine why she'd love to have a woman helping."

"Of course I can," said Cindy.

"She insists that she's completely innocent—knows nothing at all about what happened."

Cindy suddenly felt as though she were hearing an echo from the past case she'd worked on. Dalia had also proclaimed her innocence, right up to the end. It was startling for Cindy to realize that her natural trust in people was disappearing fast. Her first reaction now was to doubt and to question.

"What else do you have to do that's more important than this?" Mattheus honed in on her, refusing to let go.

"Nothing," said Cindy. "Except going back home and resuming a normal life." Even as she said it, she was aware that her life could never be normal again.

"Every life is normal if you're doing what you're supposed to," Mattheus replied.

Cindy remembered then why she respected him so. Her heart warmed.

"We'll go together. I'll back you up—you won't be alone. We can call the company C and M Investigations." He laughed. "We work well together. We're a good team."

Cindy could not deny that.

"The woman in St. Thomas needs an answer right away." Mattheus was insistent. "It's almost hurricane season there and they have to work as quickly as possible now to gather all the evidence. There are lots of lives at stake here, the woman, her family, and who knows who else? Could be a killer is on the loose."

"I hear you," said Cindy. "I hear everything."

"I'm surprised you're not jumping in."

"Give me an hour or so," Cindy said, her head suddenly reeling. It was too much for her take in all at once. She needed just a little while to walk on the beach, be with herself, and make sure this was the right decision. It was not only about working on the new case, it was about joining forces with Mattheus, creating a private detective agency. Cindy looked at him sitting there, handsome, confident, rugged. It was as if he'd always been in her life. But he hadn't. Just five months ago, she'd been married to

Clint, going off with him on their honeymoon. They'd had a home and friends they'd loved. She'd worked as an investigative reporter and had hopes of having a family one day—not tracking down killers in the Caribbean.

Cindy pushed herself away from the table and Mattheus stood up as well.

"Take as much time as you need," he said calmly.

"I'll let you know in an hour or so," she said.

Mattheus smiled and so did Cindy as the wind in the trees began blowing up, tossing Cindy's hair into her face.

"It's just that everything is happening so quickly," said Cindy, pushing her hair away.

"I know." Mattheus nodded. "New beginnings are often like that."

*

Cindy left her sandals at the edge of the beach and walked barefoot through the soft, white sand up to the water's edge. The light was fading and it was definitely cooler as the wind tossed against her face and arms. Cindy reached out her hands as if to hold onto the breeze. Would she ever get home? Would she ever again be the person she was? A few small sandpipers flew to where she was standing and looked up at her. Cindy smiled. The islands had taken everything from her, but then had also given her one gift after another, in the most unusual ways. Could it be that this was to be her new home?

Her mind flew forward to the woman on St. Thomas whose husband had been killed and dumped in a back alley. Cindy could only imagine the pain she had to be going through—the loss, confusion, and the police grilling her daily. A sense of outrage and strength flushed through Cindy's veins. She'd been there. She knew how urgently the woman needed someone she could trust. Cindy also knew that somehow she was the one to do it. She was able to navigate her way through this kind of maze, sense what was brewing beneath the surface, cut through the lies and find justice. Cindy never realized before how important justice was to her. Life wasn't worth living without it, she realized, as the water rushed up between her toes.

She took a long moment then to breathe deeply, enjoying the moment. There was no need to linger any longer. Clint's death had propelled her into a new place. She couldn't go back home and rest when another person was going through the same torture she had.

Clint would have made the same choice that she did, to fight for justice, find the culprit, stop the killer from striking again.

She had no choice. She had to say yes.

CHAPTER 2

Cindy braced herself as the sea plane dove in low for a landing. The vast stretch of shimmering blue-green water beneath them stretched out forever, calm, reassuring, and beautiful. Cindy spotted a small boat in the distance, waiting to take them to shore.

Mattheus had spent the plane ride going over his notes on the case. Cindy had spent it looking down at the water below.

"Her name is Kendra," Mattheus reminded Cindy as the plane flew closer to shore. "The wife. She's greeting us herself. A little unusual, but interesting. She must be extremely eager to meet you."

Cindy turned and looked at him. His beautiful eyes were focused on her. But Cindy merely nodded, all business at the moment.

It was a little awkward between them now, flying off into this business partnership, knowing so little about one another. It was one thing, Cindy thought, to do fabulously together on one case—but another to sustain their connection. Mattheus had left his job on the police force without hesitation. He'd been thinking about it for a while. He told Cindy he was ready to take on his own cases. And he thought it was a great idea to have a male and female detective agency; each would bring a different point of view and relate better with different people.

Cindy's stomach suddenly fell as the plane began to descend without warning. She'd never landed on the water before, or felt the movement of the plane so intimately. It reminded her of the water rides she used to go on as a kid in the amusement park.

As they landed, and floated on water, Cindy felt as if she were back in the amusement park, or in a dream. The plane bobbed gently for a few minutes until the small boat rode up to the plane.

Cindy and Mattheus got up and went to the exit, then slipped out of the plane onto the boat. Mattheus got out first and reached his hand out for Cindy, who held it tight for a few seconds. Once safely on the boat, she let go.

Mattheus laughed. "We did it. We're here." He seemed to be thoroughly enjoying both the landing and having Cindy beside him. It was a short boat ride to the shore and it felt good to be on water in the strong heat of the day. As they got closer Cindy could see a small group of people clustered together, waiting for them to arrive.

As the boat pulled up, Mattheus and Cindy got out and a tall woman with long chestnut-brown hair rushed over. She was in her fifties, slender, with large blue eyes, dressed in a paisley sundress, with several colored bracelets on her wrist.

"Finally, you're here," the woman breathed.

"Kendra Robbins?" Mattheus stepped forward.

She looked at him briefly and then turned and put the full force of her attention onto Cindy.

"I read about the amazing work you did on Grenada—and also in Barbados," she said. "I'm so thrilled you chose to come down here and help me."

"Glad to meet you," Cindy said. She was eager to get to know Kendra, but also wanted to keep things simple, not foster unrealistic expectations.

Kendra looked quickly back and forth between Cindy and Mattheus then, confused for a moment.

"We're a team," Cindy said. "C and M Investigations."

"Well," Kendra said, "there's plenty to investigate."

Cindy was glad Mattheus was with her. She could feel how they balanced each other, kept Kendra's aggression at bay.

Kendra seemed uneasy. "But I'm glad you're here. It's urgent."

"It must have been a terrible time for you," Cindy said.

"Must be? It still is," Kendra replied, rattled.

"These things have a way of going on and on," said Mattheus.

Kendra looked at him briefly with appreciation, but turned once again to Cindy.

"I'd like to take you home with me now," she said. "We can talk better there. I have a car waiting."

"Great," said Cindy.

"There's a lot to do before hurricane season," Kendra went on hurriedly, as she led them to the car. "We only have a couple of weeks to go. Once the storms come, everything is impossible, things get put on the back burner, buildings are boarded up, and evidence gets washed away. Criminals get away with everything then. I've seen it happen."

Cindy remembered that Kendra's husband was a criminal lawyer and that she had to know very well how the system worked.

"I've also seen the way the police here can zero in on one person and not bother about looking at anything else," Kendra added. "It makes it easier for them, doesn't it? They get their suspect and hound them until they crush them to a pulp." She smiled then, an odd, bitter smile, and ran her hands through her hair. Obviously she was completely frazzled from the ordeal she was going through.

An expensive car was waiting at a curb. The three of them got in and drove along winding curvy roads, then through a bustling built-up town, filled with tourists, locals, palm trees, and low buildings.

"Our home is at the other end of the town," Kendra said, as they all fell silent and looked out the window. "The police have scoured it day after day. I'm not sure exactly what they're looking for. I ask them but they don't tell me. That's why I hired you, to intercede with them for me, be an advocate. I want you to turn over every piece of unexamined evidence that I know is lying around. Find the real killer. Whoever it is, they're out there in plain view, walking around like nothing happened. I'm paying you half up front and the rest when it's over. And there'll be a big bonus on top of it when the killer's locked up in jail."

Cindy was struck by her vehemence. But Kendra had every reason to be unnerved; she'd been the main suspect since her husband was found. And she had to deal with the loss of him on top of that.

"They keep going over my home," Kendra said fitfully. "There's nothing to find there. We lived a good life. We were happy. He was a good man. No one in our home had anything to do with this. No one knows anything about it." Her voice rose as she repeated these words, which Cindy imagined she had said again and again, to no avail. The papers reported that she was still the chief suspect.

Despite herself, Cindy shivered as she remembered her friend in Grenada, Dalia, constantly telling her how happy she and her husband were, and what a good man he was. Cindy tossed her head to clear her mind. She had to realize that each situation was different. She had to give this woman a chance. Kendra and Dalia were different. It was dangerous to create suspicion so quickly based on something that had happened before. And it was easy to do, Cindy realized.

"It's easy to miss a piece of evidence," Mattheus said, "or to even realize that something's important. When you check and recheck, suddenly something hits you."

"Well, there's nothing in my home," Kendra repeated in an abrasive tone.

Cindy moved closer to Kendra in the car. "They have to believe that there's something in your home that will lead them to the killer.

It's routine to investigate the family and next of kin," she said kindly.

There was something about this woman, though, that drew doubt to her. It would be a challenge to find out who Kendra truly was and what had really gone on. And Cindy would.

The car drove through the business section quickly, past the buildings and open malls, up one hill and down another, to a neighborhood of private homes, facing out onto the ocean. The car pulled up in front of a beautiful, white stucco house, with perfect gardens in the front and a huge open porch surrounding it.

"Here we are," said Kendra.

"What a beautiful home," breathed Cindy, taking in the grandeur.

"It *was* a beautiful home," said Kendra, bitterly. "For many years. Now it's being invaded by the whole world."

Cindy was about to say something, but looked over at Mattheus, who shook his head. He was letting her know that she should back off. There was no need to soothe Kendra—they were stepping into a tangled situation and had to allow everything to be revealed. Cindy appreciated Mattheus' experience, and his sensitivity. She caught his eye and smiled at him. He smiled back as they got out of the car and walked to the front door.

Kendra's home was decorated lavishly, with large antique vases, huge plants, expensive, furniture, and amazing paintings covering the walls.

"Paul loved fine art," Kendra said, as Cindy looked slowly around. "He was a connoisseur of everything—art, food, antique vases."

"You have a wonderful collection."

"Paul earned it. He worked hard. He did well." Kendra sat down on the couch then, as if the wind were suddenly knocked out of her. "And look how he died. Horrifying."

Cindy took a deep breath and sat down beside her on the couch.

A housekeeper appeared, bringing a pitcher of water and glasses.

"Thanks, Maggie," said Kendra. "Please ask our guests what else they'd like and bring it here for them. And bring me a Marguerite, please." Then she tossed a quick look at Cindy and Mattheus. "Of course I never started drinking so early in the day, but with this incredible tension, what else is there to do?"

"Before you start drinking, we need you to talk to us," Cindy said.

"What more can I say? Seems as if every detail has been leaked to the papers."

"You're the main suspect because of the insurance policy?" Mattheus started the questioning.

"So they say," said Kendra. "Paul took the policy out about three months ago. Bad timing, to say the least. We had another policy before that for years, but suddenly Paul wanted to upgrade it. So now I have a huge insurance policy on his life and it's creating complete turmoil. Why would I kill him for money? I have plenty of money, I have this house, and I have my own tour business."

"Is that the only reason you're the suspect?" Mattheus continued.

Once again, Kendra turned to Cindy, looked at her plaintively.

"Is that the only reason? It's enough, isn't it? But, of course, there are always other matters as well. It's easier to talk about those with a woman, though," Kendra said.

"I understand," said Cindy. "Do you want Mattheus to leave the room?"

"No, he can stay here if he wants. But I'd rather talk to you. I've been dealing with men for too long now—mostly, they don't have a heart. Some even enjoy seeing us women suffer. More than you would imagine."

Mattheus flinched. "I'll take a walk on the grounds for a little while so the two of you can talk to each other."

"Thanks," said Kendra, dismissively.

Mattheus left and Cindy moved closer to Kendra.

"What do you want to tell me?" Cindy asked gently.

"I didn't do it. Why would I? Besides the damn insurance policy there's no motive anyone can find. Paul and I were happy. We did well together. We came down to the island separately, years ago. We met and fell in love right away. God knows why. Things look different when you're young. Anyway, we decided to make the island our home. Paul was a brand new lawyer, I was an art major, and decided to give tours of the island and paint. It was a lovely life. I enjoyed it. I loved living here. We built a family, had a daughter. All was going well."

"Someone had some reason to kill him, though," Cindy said softly.

Kendra's eyes filled with tears. "Who?"

"I have no idea," said Cindy. "You'll have to fill me in more on his life."

"Nobody's asked who I thought might have killed him," Kendra said in a hushed tone. "All they've kept asking me is about our marriage, and where it went wrong. It didn't go wrong. I keep telling them that."

"Never?" asked Cindy.

"A marriage is a marriage. It had ups and downs. We grew to understand each other."

Kendra's eye started twitching. "He was human like anyone. He had his flaws. They weren't a crime. He didn't deserve to die for them."

"What kind of flaws?" Cindy pursued it.

"Paul enjoyed hanging at the bars for drinks after work. It relaxed him. At first I didn't think it was a big deal. I still don't. But over the years, he did it more and more. He needed time away."

"You'll tell me which bars?" said Cindy.

"Of course I'll tell you. But so what? He had a stressful job, defending criminals and handling a damn lot of them, too. So he'd have a drink to unwind. Is that so terrible?"

"Of course not. But I need to know more about his habits."

Maggie came in with the tray carrying coffee and Marguerites. Kendra quickly reached for her drink, but Cindy stopped her.

"Later," Cindy said.

At that moment, Mattheus strolled by on the lawn in front of the large, glass windows.

Kendra put her drink down and looked at him.

"He's very gallant," Kendra said suddenly. Very handsome and very smart."

"Your husband?" asked Cindy.

"No, your friend out there. I suppose both of you have to know everything?"

"Of course we do," Cindy said.

Kendra raised her eyebrows for a moment. "Quite a team," she said. Then she reached out for her drink again, only to think better of it and put it down. "You're right; it doesn't make sense to drink so early. Besides, in a few minutes, my daughter will be coming home from school."

"The papers haven't said much about your daughter," asked Cindy, curious.

"Why should they?" Kendra was quick on the uptake. "She's in her late teens, grieving. Why drag her into this mess?"

"No reason," Cindy responded.

"Besides, she's a handful," said Kendra. "Always has been. She was close to her father, but she and I were mostly at odds. Not so unusual for mothers and teenage daughters."

"So I've heard," said Cindy. "I look forward to meeting her."

Kendra shrugged. "Whatever," she said.

"Anything else you want to tell me now?" asked Cindy.

Kendra sat up stiffly in her chair. Cindy could see this was hard for her. She resented every minute of it, was brittle and proud. It wasn't her way to speak freely to strangers.

"What I wanted to say is something simple, but it hurts like hell. I told it to the cops, but it didn't make a dent on them. They laughed in my face."

"What is it?" said Cindy.

"Paul stayed out of town a few nights every week. Said he was in St. Croix. He had cases there, but he also liked to gamble. It was his one weak spot, if you can call it that. He told me he stayed in St. Croix for his work, but I often wondered if something else drew him."

"The gambling?"

"I grew to wonder if he had a woman."

Cindy took a deep, quick breath. It made sense.

"It's not that unusual, you know," Kendra added quickly, surprised at Cindy's reaction. "We'd been together for almost twenty years. It wasn't that he wasn't good to me. He was. By a woman, I mean a mistress. Something on the side, not important. His murder could have something to do with that. These island women out here get crazy, start dreaming about all kinds of things."

The door to living room opened and Mattheus walked in and came over to Kendra.

Clearly, he was eager to get to the next step.

"I think it's important for us to check in to the police station now, let them know we've arrived, and see what else they have for us to do. We'll all have plenty of time to talk to each other, fill in the details."

Cindy knew it was time to move on for now. She needed to get the name of the bar Paul hung out at, and more information about his work on St. Croix.

A strange pall came over Kendra's face as the two of them got up to leave. "You just arrived and now you're leaving," she said in an odd tone.

"We need to get filled in on as much as we can as soon as possible," Cindy said. "We'll be back in a little while. You're not alone."

"Wrong again," Kendra echoed in a husky voice. "I'm completely alone. More alone than you can ever imagine. And no one even really knows."

CHAPTER 3

The police station was located in a mid-sized stucco building off the main road. A wide entranceway surrounded by a fence, bordered by palm trees, led up to the main entrance. Little geckos jumped happily along the fence, peering out at visitors unsuspectingly. Mattheus had notified the police that he and Cindy would be arriving and had been hired to work on the case.

When Cindy and Mattheus walked in, a few policemen were sitting at desks, a few others gathered in the rear talking. At first no one looked up.

Mattheus walked up to the policeman at the front desk. "Mattheus—private investigator," he said and extended his hand.

The officer at the desk looked up and took Mattheus in. In a flash, he decided that he liked him and extended his hand. "Heard you were coming. Fred Brayton," he said and took Mattheus' hand.

Mattheus, an experienced cop, felt at home with the police, and the guy probably felt it. Cindy watched the two of them size each other up favorably.

"Welcome to the island," Brayton continued. A few of the other cops looked up and came over.

"This is my partner, Cindy," Mattheus said, including her.

Fred Brayton smiled a wide smile, showing huge white teeth. "Now that's what I call a fine business," he said.

Some of the other cops looked at Cindy briefly. One raised his eyes, surprised. Clearly they were not accustomed to women detectives down here on the islands. She saw she would have to earn their respect.

Brayton got up from behind his desk, turning entirely to Mattheus. "We checked you out when we heard you were coming," he said. "The guys down in Grenada only had the best things to say about you."

Mattheus flushed. He seemed to like being recognized among his peers.

"So, let's go inside and talk a few minutes," Mattheus said. "You can fill us in on the details."

Brayton threw a quick look at Cindy, wondering if she were coming too.

"Cindy's done some fantastic work," Mattheus interjected immediately.

"Beginner's luck," Cindy heard another tall, muscular cop mutter under his breath.

"We're lucky to have Cindy on board," Mattheus said definitively.

Brayton seemed taken aback at Mattheus' vehemence; so did a few of the other cops. They stopped and looked at her hard. Cindy felt the band of brotherhood between them that naturally kept a woman at bay.

"The widow requested a woman detective to work with her on her case," Mattheus continued.

"The *widow*?" Brayton laughed in a mocking tone. "Wouldn't exactly call the little wife a widow."

"Why not?" Mattheus asked at once, alerted.

"Let's all go in and sit down," Brayton said, nodding in Cindy's direction, inviting her to join them as well. "There's a lot to cover."

He led them and a few other cops down through a long hallway, into a meeting room with a round table, ceiling fan, and huge coffee machine in the corner, with paper cups piled near it.

Brayton went over to the coffee maker and began pouring coffee into some cups.

"You take yours with or without milk and sugar?" he asked Cindy first.

"Milk and sugar," said Cindy.

"I'll have mine black," Mattheus said.

Brayton came back with the coffee and the tall, muscular cop went to a file, yanked it open, and pulled out some papers. Then he came back to the table and sat beside them. Two other cops joined them around the table as well.

They all sat quietly for a moment and drank their coffee until Brayton broke the silence. "This lady isn't exactly what we call a grieving widow. From the way things look to us now—we got the killer."

Cindy breathed in swiftly. Shocking, she thought. Case closed in their minds.

"Show me what you have," said Mattheus.

Brayton riffled through some papers with one hand and he gulped more coffee with the other.

"Okay, here's what we got. As you probably know, the hubby took out a two-million-dollar insurance policy in her name, just three months before he got killed."

Mattheus raised his eyebrows. "We heard. That's a lot of cash."

"Just three months before," the big muscular, cop chimed in. "Tell me why?"

"Good question," said Mattheus.

"But why would she be so stupid to kill him such a short time after?" Cindy asked. "It's too obvious."

The big, muscular cop closed his eyes until they were almost slits and peered at Cindy.

"Nothing is obvious to someone who gets it in their minds to kill," he muttered. "They all think they can do anything they want and no one will catch them. I know these killers inside and out. They think they got a right to snuff out a life at the drop of a dime. It gives them a thrill."

Brayton laughed a little. "Nojo has his theories. He's a great cop, almost never wrong."

Nojo seemed to like that. He cocked his head to the side. "I can smell a killer ten miles away."

"Sounds like you think the case is closed." Cindy took him on.

Nojo grinned. "Your little lady has got a feisty nature," he said to Mattheus.

Mattheus shook his head. "She likes to hear all the details."

Cindy didn't like being spoken of as a little lady. She realized Mattheus was standing up for her, but she could do it for herself as well. This crazy cop, Nojo, made her uneasy. He seemed to have a vendetta.

"Okay, what else do you have?" Mattheus wanted to move forward.

"No alibi," Nojo broke in. "Time of death was about five thirty p.m. Where was she then? This is what will get her! She said she was at home. Really? This was a working lady. Every other day she was out at work, leading tours of the island. How come this particular day she was home? She said she didn't feel well, had bad dreams all night before. I bet she did." As Nojo spoke his mouth grew wet with saliva. He tasted victory and an easy one at that.

"What else?" asked Cindy, impatient.

"Hold on a minute and listen," Nojo said. "Did anyone see her at home that day? No one. Her housekeeper was off for the day. Convenient. Her daughter didn't happen to come home after school. She decided to spend the afternoon away. Very, very convenient. It doesn't take an idiot to know that none of this adds up."

"And where's the husband at that time, usually?" asked Mattheus.

"Usually the poor jerk's out working late, or out of town on a case. But that's beside the point now. What I'm asking is how come the day he was killed his daughter didn't come home?"

"She could have had her reasons," said Cindy.

Nojo closed his eyes completely. "Everyone has their reasons," he said. "But do they add up? Or are they just building a noose to hang themselves in?"

Cindy didn't like him. She felt that he lived off these tragedies, expected them, practically hoped for them.

"And besides that, the daughter, Nell, is weird," Nojo continued. "I asked her where were you that afternoon? She said she stayed late in school to study. You even getting the drift of this bullshit? Now this fish is starting to stink worse than before." He turned to Cindy. "One piece of crap after another."

"Why wouldn't she be studying late in school?" Cindy asked.

"Not something she usually does! And no one happened to see her there either."

Brayton took a long breath. So did Mattheus. None of it looked good.

"She's covering for the mother. It's obvious," Nojo belted out.

Nothing felt obvious to Cindy. She refused to go along with easy, snap conclusions.

"You want another detail?" Brayton was joining in. "We found out that Kendra bought an incredibly expensive ruby necklace, about a week before the murder. And what happened to it? You can't find the piece anywhere in the house. When we showed her the receipt for the sale, she swore she put the necklace in her house safe. When we opened it, there's nothing there. She said she had no idea what happened to it. And why'd she even buy it for? She wouldn't tell us. It doesn't add up. None of it does."

"No, it doesn't," Mattheus agreed.

"It's all circumstantial," said Cindy. "So far I haven't heard any direct link between Kendra and the murder. Do you have any evidence or DNA?"

Nojo stood up at that and hovered over Cindy. "We put plenty of criminals down on this island with less circumstantial evidence than this."

Cindy shivered.

"You got some better ideas?" Nojo's tone was becoming threatening.

Mattheus stood up between them. "We've been called down here to investigate," he said. "We've got to look at everything."

"Like what?" Nojo's eyes narrowed into slits again.

"Paul was a criminal lawyer," Cindy spoke up. "Was there someone he defended who might have had a grudge against him? A case he lost? Someone who got sent to jail?"

"That's a good point," said Mattheus.

"Nah," said Nojo, "this guy knew what he was doing. He had a great reputation. His clients loved him."

"But someone might not have," said Cindy. "Did you check any cases he lost? The person might have felt ripped off. Might have spent time sitting in jail dreaming of revenge?"

"I hate it when women think they know everything," Nojo muttered under his breath.

Brayton bit his lower lip. "Not a bad idea." He seemed a little embarrassed not to have thought of it himself. "Okay, we'll look into it."

"I'll give you a hand with that," said Mattheus.

Brayton looked up at him, grateful. "This guy you got here," he said to Cindy, "is a good guy."

"I'll second that," said Nojo.

Cindy felt at a loss as to what to say. She didn't *have* Mattheus, they worked together.

Mattheus stepped in easily to smooth everything out. "We're business partners," he said to the guys. "And I'm equally lucky. Cindy's a terrific partner."

Cindy felt grateful, but uneasy as well. She'd stumbled into a male world here that had no room for her. That's fine, she thought. Mattheus will handle this part, and I'll take on other aspects of this crime. There's more than enough to go around.

"Before we check in to our hotel," Mattheus said, "we'd like to look over the crime scene."

"No need for it," said Nojo, haltingly. "It's been combed back and forth. The guy was found lying in a pool of blood. Medical examiner found stab marks all over his body. Lots of them."

Cindy closed her eyes. Just the thought of it made her feel woozy.

"What's wrong, sweetheart?" Nojo laughed. "We haven't found the weapon yet. But when there's that many stab marks it's a crime of passion. The person who did it hated his guts."

"Let them look," Brayton broke in. "Another pair of eyes can see something else."

"Great," said Mattheus. "Tell us how to get to there and gain access."

"You got it," said Brayton, obviously happy to have Mattheus on the team. "But don't let the little lady go down there alone. You can never tell who’s lurking around. That place has a way of attracting dangerous scum and buzzards, especially after dark.”

CHAPTER 4

There was about an hour left of light in the day, enough for them to familiarize themselves with the crime scene. Even though it was no longer cordoned off, Mattheus wanted to inspect every inch of it.

"The crime scene is always the richest source of information," he said to Cindy as they walked along the streets that were bursting with people, life, color, and smells. They passed by open shopping stalls that lined the streets, buyers displaying their wares; fruits, jams, nuts, paintings, straw hats, scarves, clothes hanging out, waving slightly in the breeze. The area had something of the feel of a carnival, but with naturalness about it. Some tourists stood around inspecting the goods; others bargained for the best prices. Life was lived there, wide open for all to see. There were ample stores filled with everything from T-shirts to crafts to luxury items that lured you in. Charlotte Amalie, long the center of commerce, offers more than just shopping opportunities. The history of the island could be seen in its stores that used to be warehouses or merchants' homes, centuries ago.

"This island used to be controlled by the Danish," said Mattheus. "If we took a short walk, we'd end up in Fort Christian. That used to be a military construction that's been converted to a museum where you can learn all about the island's history and culture."

Cindy suddenly felt a wave of exhaustion flood over her. There seemed to be no end to the twists and turns, people, and human affairs that called out for help and resolution. She stopped for a moment and stood still, taking it all in. How did she get here with Mattheus, almost a stranger, on what could actually be a dangerous expedition? she wondered. Mattheus seemed confident, happy, and on high alert, though, as he walked beside her, full of curiosity. When Cindy stopped in her tracks, he looked surprised.

"I need to take a moment," she said.

"For what?"

"It's a lot to absorb all at once."

"Of course it is," he said, and unexpectedly, put his arm around her and gave her a quick hug. "You've been catapulted from one world into another." Then he took his arm away.

Catapulted was a good word for it. Cindy appreciated Mattheus' understanding and also the quick show of support.

"Things will start to fall into place," he said. "They always do. The beginning can be confusing. A whirl of events, conflicting ideas. That's the fun part too," and he grinned.

Cindy saw how much he enjoyed what he was doing. It excited him, stimulated him—he was made for this life.

"This place is very different from Grenada," Cindy said, looking around. She was used to long, quiet afternoons, surrounded by sun and sea, driving from one lead to another, interviewing people privately, dwelling on what they'd said. Here she was thrust in the middle of a throbbing, noisy, crowded city, where life moved quickly to its own beat.

"Different is good," said Mattheus. "Too much of the same thing puts you to sleep."

Cindy laughed. She enjoyed the fact that Mattheus often surprised her with his unexpected insights which went way beyond the simple facts they were dealing with. In that way, he reminded her of Clint. She remembered the wonderful conversations she and Clint used to have. They'd talk all night and into the morning. Clint had also loved taking the largest perspective possible on whatever was going on. Cindy took a moment to wonder how Clint would react to what she was doing, and whether in some way he was with her now.

"Let's move on," Mattheus urged her. "We'll have time to dwell on things later. We've got to get to the crime scene while there's still light. And before the storms come in."

Cindy wondered how much could possibly be left. "It's an open street now," she remarked. "People walk through it every day."

"True," said Mattheus, smiling. Cindy saw that he was pleased by her comment. "But the kind of thing we're looking for won't be brushed away so easily. The police checked the scene carefully in the beginning for that kind of evidence."

"What exactly are we looking for?" Cindy asked him.

"We'll know when we get there," said Mattheus. "The place will speak to us. When you get to a crime scene, especially one that's been gone over, the best way is to get real quiet, and let your eyes scan the place. Don't focus on every little thing you're seeing, just let your mind take it all in. It can take a few days sometimes before you realize what you saw. Then, someone says something, you make a connection, and suddenly it pops into your mind."

Cindy liked that. She loved it when Mattheus showed a layer of sensitivity that she didn't normally see. She also loved learning the trade from him. He was a generous mentor.

They picked up their pace and walked briskly on toward the end of that street and then turned right into a narrow lane, behind a shopping stall. The two of them stopped at the entrance, automatically, at the same moment, and peered in.

The lane was narrow, shaded, and curved slightly as it led to the back of the street. It was also filled with a strong aroma of smoke and meat cooking. Cindy could see a few lizards skittering by and hear the call of birds. She shuddered. This was a perfect place to dump a body, she thought.

"I'm not surprised," Mattheus said.

"At what?" asked Cindy.

"This is a natural spot to dump a body," he said. "But it's also a spot where you'd know it would be found. Whoever dumped the guy here didn't want him hidden. They wanted him to be found. They probably want to be found as well."

Cindy remembered reading years ago that all criminals had a secret yearning to be discovered, to pay for their crimes, make atonement. That was why jailhouse confessions were so common. She thought about that for a long time. She'd always been fascinated by the workings of justice and how, deep down, each person craved it, no matter what they had done.

Now, she and Mattheus approached the actual spot where the body had been found and Mattheus stopped and bent over. Stains of blood could still be seen soaked into some of the stones.

"Can't ever get all the blood up," Mattheus said. "They left a lot here. Surprised they didn't find fingerprints or DNA that could link them to the killer."

Somehow it didn't surprise Cindy. She felt there was a different route through which this crime would be solved.

Mattheus took photos of the stones on the street, lizards, walls, the angle of the sunlight. They walked together slowly up and down the lane, and then suddenly, something caught Cindy's eye. It was over against the far wall, a scrap of paper the wind must have blown over, that got stuck between two rocks. She went over to it immediately and slowly pulled the paper out. A few words were scrawled on it in a shaky hand. By now they had faded and were hard to make out.

"Look at this," she said to Mattheus.

He turned abruptly. “What?”

“This paper. There are a few words written on it.”

Mattheus walked over and looked. “Doesn’t look like it says anything.”

“It does.” Cindy kept scrutinizing the paper, then folded it up neatly and put it in her bag.

Mattheus smiled. “We can’t grab at straws.”

“It’s a strange handwriting,” said Cindy. “Did you notice the strange slope of the letters, the shakiness of the hand? They’re calling out for attention. Whoever wrote this was in a bad state of mind.”

Mattheus was taken aback. “How do you know about that?”

“It’s amazing what you can tell about a person from the way they write,” said Cindy. “It’s a giveaway if you know what to look for. I want to compare this to Kendra’s hand. And maybe others.”

“Smart,” said Mattheus and laughed. “What about me? Did you ever analyze my handwriting?”

Cindy laughed as well. She’d never thought about it. “Not yet,” she said.

“I’d better be careful,” Mattheus chuckled.

“What are you hiding?” Cindy laughed.

At that moment a large, black bird flew over them, cawing loudly. They both looked up swiftly and watched it fly by. Standing here at the crime scene, she was flooded with all kinds of information, floating around in her mind. She began to wonder about Kendra, her true fears and desires, her hidden characters, compulsions, and secrets. If you knew how to read a person, nothing was truly hidden.

“The question is why the killer chose this particular spot,” Mattheus murmured as he scanned it. “They might have some particular connection to it, could have been a regular visitor.”

“They planned this out carefully,” Cindy mused. “This isn’t a spot you come to randomly. The body was heavy, it had to take at least two people to carry it here.”

“Reports claim the murder took place on this spot,” Mattheus reminded her.

“How could it have?” Cindy shook her head. “Paul died at around five thirty p.m. It’s too busy and crowded here for this to happen during the day and no one notice.”

“Someone could have noticed and gotten out of here fast. People don’t like to get involved in trouble. Especially the locals,” said Mattheus. “In fact, someone could have been paid off, to keep their mouth shut. “I’m going to talk to the locals and merchants.”

"The police did already," said Cindy.

"Maybe? But people don't usually talk to police. They don't want trouble, it's bad for business to call attention to something like this. With us, it will be different. We're just simple folk."

Cindy walked back and forth slowly then, tuning into the overall energy, listening for an unheard vibration that could lead her to something. As she walked her eye caught a little hole at the end of the lane. At first it looked inconsequential, like a pocket of dirt. She went over and looked in. To her surprise, there was a tiny cloth wrapper buried inside. Cindy leaned in, pulled it out, and opened it quickly. Inside the wrapper was one round earring made of gold. It was a small and strangely shaped earring for pierced ears.

"Look at this, Mattheus," she called out.

Mattheus came right over. Cindy held the squiggly earring up.

"What's that?" he asked.

"I found it in this hole."

Mattheus looked at the earring. "Good work," he said, "but any number of people could have dropped it there. This is a shopping thoroughfare."

"That's true," said Cindy. "But it was wrapped in its own dark cloth wrapper."

"One earring?" said Mattheus.

"Just this," she said, holding it up to the light and then putting it into her pocketbook beside the scraggly paper.

"The killer wouldn't have dumped the body and then taken the time to deposit this earring in a mud hole," Mattheus said. "It doesn't make sense."

"Nothing makes sense," Cindy responded, "until we find all the pieces."

Another large bird flew over them again, howling into the early evening.

*

As the light faded and evening drew in, Cindy and Mattheus headed for a taxi to take them to their hotel.

The taxi drove slowly, allowing them to unwind and take in the sights of the island in twilight. Their hotel was located on the top of a hill, overlooking the bay. The beach near it was white, sandy, and inviting, one of the most popular on the island. Sailing and snorkeling trips left from the dock. Jet skis were available and the hotel's restaurants were great spots for lunch or dinner.

Cindy was hungry, but she was also a little apprehensive. This was going to be their first night on the island. For a brief moment, she thought about how nice it would be to spend more time with Mattheus, but also felt how important it was to keep things clear right from the start.

The taxi drove up the winding hill to their hotel, which was lined with trees, flowers, and little benches. They got out, paid the driver, and went to register. Kendra had arranged to have their luggage dropped off at the hotel as soon as they arrived, so they could spend the afternoon investigating. Now, they registered and received two rooms, adjacent to one another. The man at the desk smiled as he gave them the keys and looked from one to the other.

"Do you need separate bell boys to take up the luggage?" He grinned.

"Yes, please. We're going to have dinner in the restaurant first," Mattheus said.

Mattheus' smooth finessing of the awkward moment eased Cindy's mind. Obviously, he, too, wanted to make sure things were clear between them. Cindy appreciated that and then recalled the afternoon on Grenada when someone had told her that Mattheus was unavailable. She remembered wondering why someone as handsome and engaging as he was would want to be alone.

Now, they went to the dining room out on the veranda overlooking the bay and ordered. The moment the waiter left, Mattheus immediately picked up where they left off, discussing the case.

"I think the best idea is for us to split up," Mattheus said immediately.

Despite herself, Cindy's stomach lurched.

"In the morning we'll go in different directions. This way we can cover twice as much ground."

The waiter brought their wine on a tray made of pink seashells.

Mattheus immediately raised his glass for a toast.

"To the beginning of a wonderful business," he said. "May we help all those we come into contact with."

"I'll drink to that," said Cindy, raising the glass to her lips slowly, enjoying the coolness of the drink. Then she suddenly looked up and saw Mattheus' eyes gazing into hers. Their glance touched and held for a moment and then they both quickly looked away.

"What do you plan to investigate in the morning?" Cindy asked, bringing them both back to focus.

Mattheus seemed to appreciate it. “Thinking of running over to St. Croix,” he said. “The police reports and Kendra mentioned that Paul spent time on St. Croix, both on business and at the casinos. I thought I’d check out the casinos first. They could be a treasure trove of information, especially if he was a regular. And from the looks of the reports, the police didn’t spend much time doing that.”

“Great idea,” said Cindy.

“And you?” Mattheus asked.

“I’m going to visit the bars he hung out at. Kendra said she thought he might have had a mistress. It’s an important thing to look into next.”

“Very important,” said Mattheus, draining the glass of wine quickly. “You have the name of the bars?”

“Yes,” said Cindy.

Mattheus leaned back and then frowned for a moment.

“Something wrong?” asked Cindy.

He shook his head lightly. “No, of course not. I just don’t love the idea of you hanging at these bars here alone.”

Cindy was startled and smiled. She loved Mattheus’ protectiveness, but this was a murder case they’d come down to solve. Who said it would be easy? Who said it would be safe?

CHAPTER 5

Mattheus was relieved to be getting away from St. Thomas for a couple of days. He needed time alone. He wasn't used to being with someone as much as he'd been with Cindy these past few days. It took some getting used to. Not that there was anything wrong with her. Far from it. She was beautiful, graceful, considerate, smart as hell, anything a guy could wish for. That made it even rougher.

These past few years since Shelly'd died, he'd learned to live on his own and like it—perhaps he'd become too independent. It had served him well, though, and he wasn't exactly sure why he'd decided to mess with the life he'd been living. He did know though that he'd been running out of steam, doing the same thing over and over, on the police force. He'd always wanted his own agency. When Mattheus met Cindy, the pieces just started coming together. He felt if he didn't act on it right away, she'd go home and slip away from him.

Mattheus took a deep breath now as he boarded the little plane over to St. Croix. It was a good move to go there. The guy who'd been killed had spent a lot of time on St. Croix—especially in the casinos. It was virgin territory for the investigation. Mattheus was a little surprised that the police hadn't covered that ground more carefully, but he knew how investigations down on the islands went—slow and easy—everyone took their time. More than that, once they had a suspect they usually zeroed in on that. It was easier, more efficient. The guys on the police force down here were always characters. For a second he thought about not boarding the plane, but going back to check on Cindy. That was nuts. They were down here as partners. She could hold her own. She'd come down alone to Grenada. Hell, she'd even solved her own husband's murder in Barbados by herself, way before they'd met.

The plane lifted easily and took him across the beautiful waters to the neighboring island. He could see some boats out already, dotting the seas, people jumping off them, snorkeling. Life down on these islands could be like a dream—unless you woke up suddenly and found someone lying in a pool of blood.

The plane landed in Turtle Lake, close to the casino Paul used to gamble in. It was a well-known spot which drew all kinds of visitors, tourists and regulars. The place was open around the clock, day and night blending into one.

Before he went to the casino, Mattheus spent time on the island walking around, getting something to eat, picking up the paper, letting the time go by. The people he needed to talk to at the casino wouldn't be there until later. As he walked, he rolled the facts of the case over in his mind. So far, it didn't look good for Kendra. But the question of how she got Paul into the alleyway bothered Mattheus. It bothered everyone. If she killed him there, it would had to have been an impulsive killing, in the heat of rage. If it was premeditated, she could have found a quieter, less flashy place. So far no weapon had been found either, though they'd searched her place from top to bottom. Of course, she could have buried the knife.

Mattheus needed more information about her, about Paul, their life together. At first glance she seemed to be a tough, arrogant woman, not someone you'd naturally have sympathy for. The papers presented a picture of a good life and perfect marriage. These picture-perfect marriages irritated him. He didn't believe them for a second. No marriage was perfect, and when it pretended to be, trouble always lay ahead.

When the time came, Mattheus walked over to the casino and went in the front door. Then he headed for the restaurant to fill up with black coffee.

There were all kinds of people floating around inside, some bleary-eyed, some sullen looking, others staring blindly at the slot machines. Mattheus began drifting around, then went to a dealer and mentioned Paul's name.

"You know the guy?"

"Sits over there." The guy motioned to a table off at the side of the room for poker. "He'll probably be in, in an hour or two."

"Not today," said Mattheus.

The guy looked up at him.

"When did you last see him?" Mattheus continued.

The guy shrugged. "He's here all the time. I don't keep a record. Probably last saw him a day or two ago."

Mattheus grimaced. The harsh lights in the casino blurred the distinction between night and day. It was easy to lose track of time.

"He was killed a week ago," said Mattheus, waiting to see how he would respond.

The dealer's jaw hung open. "You're kidding me!"

"It was in all the papers."

The dealer backed off. "Don't get much chance to look at the papers these days. Jesus Christ."

"You knew the guy?"

"Everybody knows him. He's been a staple in this place for years. Who the hell killed him? And for what?"

"That's what I'm trying to find out," said Mattheus.

"You a cop?"

"Detective. Specially called in on the case."

"Jesus, sweet God," the dealer muttered. "I'll tell you one thing, there was absolutely no reason to take this guy out. He was a fair guy—paid his debts. Never tricked a soul."

"You sure about that?" Mattheus looked at him quizzically.

"Of course I'm sure."

"I need the truth," said Mattheus.

"Then get away from me and get the hell over to that table there. It's where he sat. The guys over there played with him. I just saw him in passing."

Mattheus knew he'd been harder on him than necessary. But bum leads wasted time, and pissed him off. So many people pretended they knew it all, couldn't bring themselves to just say they had no idea what was going on.

Mattheus ambled over toward the table where the guy said Paul hung out. It was medium size, situated in a half-lit section of the place. There were about five or six others sitting there, looking at their cards. Rolls of green, red, and yellow chips were piled in front of all of them. As soon as Mattheus sat down, the dealer immediately looked over at him.

"I'm a friend of Paul's," Mattheus remarked loudly. Everyone at the table put their cards down and looked up at him.

"What kind of friend?" the dealer asked, right away. He was a short, heavy guy, half bald, with hanging jowls.

"I'm here to help him," Mattheus said.

"Too late for that," the dealer said gruffly.

The guy sitting next to Mattheus poked Mattheus in the ribs softly, as if to say *shut up*.

He was tall and thin with red hair and big eyes; he bit the corner of his lip.

"The guy was killed a couple of weeks ago, week ago," the dealer continued, as a pall fell over the table.

"Any idea who?" Mattheus jumped right in.

"If I knew that I'd be right at the police." The dealer thumped his short hand on the hard table. "He was one of us. No one here did it." And he looked at Mattheus with fire in his eyes.

"There was no reason for it."

"There's never a reason to die," said Mattheus.

"Yeah, but there's always a reason when it's murder," the dealer retorted.

"Someone had something against him." Mattheus wouldn't let up.

"No one I knew," the dealer insisted. "He lived his life straight up."

The guy next to Mattheus poked him again. Mattheus turned his attention to him.

"Hi," Mattheus said to him, extending his hand. "Mattheus King."

"Roomey Burke." The guy looked over and took Mattheus' hand.

"Okay, deal," someone else at the table called out. The conversation was over. It seemed like they'd all been through this for a while now and wanted to move on.

"Mind giving me a minute or two?" Mattheus asked Roomey. "We could sit over there and talk."

"Sure," said Roomey, and put his cards down. "A minute or two."

"Deal," one of the guys at the table insisted.

Roomey and Mattheus got up, walked a few feet to a lounge with some comfortable couches and chairs, and sat down.

Roomey was a strange mixture of elegance and anxiety. Out of place here, Mattheus thought. "You knew him well?"

"Very," said Roomey.

Mattheus looked at him more carefully and wondered why. What could they have had in common?

"It was a shock to everyone," said Roomey. "Especially me. I talked to him almost every day."

Mattheus was surprised to hear that. This could be an important find. "You're a lawyer, too?" Mattheus asked.

"Architect. We both live in St. Thomas and spend a couple of days here during the week. Takes the pressure off, to a degree."

"Suppose it does," said Mattheus.

"I knew him well. I know the family," Roomey continued.

This guy had to be a treasure trove of information, Mattheus thought.

"Police say the wife did it." Mattheus was curious what his reaction would be.

Roomey smiled a strange, pained smile. "That's ridiculous," he said definitively. "She's innocent."

"You sure?"

"She's a terrific woman." His eyes flared a bit.

"How do you know that?"

"Just take it from me."

"I can't just take it. I need solid information," Mattheus mumbled, but loud enough so he could hear him.

Roomey obviously didn't like being pressed. He pulled back a little and tapped his fingers against each other. "What are you? A detective of some kind?"

"Yes," said Mattheus.

"Really?" Roomey's eyes opened at that. "Thought you were a reporter or something, possibly a family member who flew in to help. None of them even came to the funeral, you know. Paul and Kendra both have family back in the states who wrote them off years ago, when they got married and settled here. He never even introduced her to his family. That's probably why they moved away in the first place," Roomey said bitterly. "You can't blame them."

No, you can't, Mattheus thought. That was a lousy deal, no family coming down to the funeral. No family standing up for Kendra either. Lots of people who'd settled down here on the islands had some kind of story like that. Mattheus wondered if that was why Roomey was down here as well.

"Help me out with this," Mattheus said.

"I've become like family to them now," Roomey said softly. "Kendra's beautiful, smart." His face flushed as he spoke.

Mattheus looked at him intently. "Why are the police pouncing on Kendra?" Mattheus asked.

"To avoid looking further," Roomey said. "I've seen it happen over and over. Especially down here. It's easy, next of kin—especially with a big insurance policy."

"Are they focusing on her to cover something up?" Mattheus asked.

"Could be," said Roomey. "I hadn't really thought of that. It can be pretty corrupt down this way. Paul and Kendra had money, position, a beautiful daughter. People get weird about all that."

"Weird enough to kill?" asked Mattheus.

"All kinds of idiots floating around, who knows what they were thinking? Could be someone got jealous? Or maybe had a vendetta with Kendra?"

Mattheus wondered what they would have a vendetta with Kendra about, but let Roomey keep talking.

"Look, I'm not the detective. You are," Roomey said. "I stepped over here because I wanted to help out."

"I appreciate that," said Mattheus. "Would you give me your card so we can keep in touch?" Mattheus said. "Seems like you have lots of answers."

Roomey had no problem with that. He gave Mattheus his card quickly. "Got plenty of questions, too," he said.

"Before I go now," said Mattheus, "is there anything else you can think of? Any little detail at all?"

Roomey still looked troubled. "Well, there is one thing." His voice dropped an octave, and it was hard to hear. "There was a private poker game each week between a bunch of us fellas, high stakes. Much too high, if you know what I mean." He smiled unevenly, his face going out of whack. "Paul loved the game. He was good too, much too good if you asked me. That guy had the brain of an eel, slipping inside of cracks and corners, able to figure anything out. That's what he lived for. Beating the odds."

"He lost a lot?" Mattheus was fascinated.

"Just the opposite." Roomed smiled again. "He cleaned up almost every time."

"Cheated?"

"Nah, I told you, he had the brain of an eel."

"So why the hell did you guys keep playing with him?"

Roomey licked his lips. "The thrill of the game. It was worth it. I could afford it, but another guy couldn't. He was in debt to Paul, big time. He just couldn't stop playing. His debt kept growing. Paul liked lording it over him, having the guy cringe around him. Made Paul feel powerful."

This was a completely different angle. Mattheus had to find out who the guy was, check him out. His bill could have gotten too big for him. What better way to get rid of it than to take out Paul?

"Thanks for telling me this," said Mattheus. "Can you give me the guy's name?"

"Nah," said Roomey. "That's private."

"This is a murder investigation." Mattheus grimaced.

Roomey nodded. "I know. I can't give you his name, but I can tell you which guy in the casino knows who the players were in the game. There weren't so many of us. It won't be hard to track him down."

This was one crafty guy. Mattheus was grateful. Obviously Roomey cared about his friend. "Anything else?" Mattheus pressed on.

Roomey still looked troubled. "Well, sooner or later you're gonna hear this. Paul and Kendra were married a lot of years. She got a little lonely at the end. It wasn't a big deal. Natural, if you asked me. Probably inevitable."

It *was* natural, Mattheus thought, to get lonely, even after years with someone at your side. Mattheus suddenly liked the guy and respected him.

"How did you know she was lonely?" Mattheus wanted a little more.

"We talked a little bit from time to time. I'd call to talk to him and she'd pick up the phone."

"She *said* she was lonely?"

Roomey got jittery. "Of course not. I just felt it. She'd hang on too long, want to talk more and more. That's all I noticed."

"And where were you the day Paul died?" Mattheus couldn't help but ask.

Roomey slithered in his chair. "You've got to be kidding."

"It's routine," said Mattheus, "nothing more. How did you hear about it?"

Roomey just smiled oddly. "Everyone who knew him was asked what they were doing that afternoon but me. I was waiting for the time someone would ask me."

"It's routine," Mattheus repeated.

"Sure, I realize that. There was a design show at the museum in town that day. My drawings and models were exhibited at it. I was there all day. So were lots of others."

Convenient, thought Mattheus. "And Kendra wasn't there?"

"Usually she attends every year, but this time she woke up feeling lousy. Rotten luck for her, though." His brow curled and his eyes glossed over. You could see how much it bothered him.

"You married yourself?" asked Mattheus.

Roomey drew back then, and tightened his jaw. He didn't like the turn of the conversation.

"I'm not the marrying kind," he said finally, between closed lips. "Never have been. Never will."

Mattheus looked at him, on alert.

Roomey felt it immediately. "Is that another crime?" he asked, jittery.

It was something in the tone of his voice that put Mattheus off. "Of course not," said Mattheus.

"How about you?" Roomey turned the tables then. "You the marrying kind?"

Mattheus drew back. "Once I was," said Mattheus. "At a different time."

"Anyone in the picture now?" Roomey asked, interested.

“No,” said Mattheus, “no one,” as the muscle under his left eye started to twitch.

CHAPTER 6

Cindy slipped into a fitted black sleeveless dress, brushed her hair loose over her shoulders, grabbed a small, sparkly evening bag, and went to the bar that Paul hung out at after work. It was downtown, on a wide street lined with clubs, bars, and topless night spots. The front entrance of the bar was hidden by a long purple awning, covered with shining lights. There were pots of flowers outside, and you could hear the music of a live jazz band playing inside.

When she walked in, people were speaking freely to each other, drinking, laughing. Cindy saw some guys at the bar look up at her admiringly. It would take about three minutes, Cindy figured, to get a date for dinner and beyond.

Cindy thought about Mattheus for a moment and smiled. She wondered what he was doing in the casino, if he was getting useful tips. She also wondered how he would react seeing her here now. There was a kind of freedom she felt with him away, but he was also on her mind.

Cindy went to the bar, took an empty seat, and ordered a rum and coke. The bartender was a local, in his mid-forties, with warm eyes and a welcoming smile. Probably a good person to start talking to, Cindy thought, especially as this was one of Paul's regular haunts.

"Did you happen to know Paul Robbins?" Cindy started lightly.

The bartender stopped and frowned. "Of course. Who didn't know Paul?" He stared at Cindy. "Why do you ask?"

A woman sitting next to Cindy, with long, flowing chestnut-brown hair, a low-cut dress, and bright red lipstick, overheard and broke in. "You looking for Paul Robbins?" she asked.

"Yes," said Cindy.

"Well, it's too late, honey," the woman went on.

"That's a hell of a way to talk about my friend," the bartender interrupted, offended.

The woman shrugged. "What did I say? Just that it's too late."

"What would Paul do if he heard you?" The bartender's eyes were flashing. "Is that how he deserves to be talked about?"

"He can't hear anything anymore," she said and turned on her barstool to Cindy. "He's gone."

"I realize," said Cindy.

"You realize?" The bartender looked really perturbed.

"I came down to the island to help with the case," Cindy said softly. She liked the bartender and wanted help any way she could get it.

"Who are you?" the woman asked. Apparently she'd taken a liking to Cindy.

"Cindy Blaine," Cindy said,

"A cop?" The woman's eyes opened wide.

"Private detective," said Cindy.

"Working for who?" The bartender was riveted.

"Kendra Robbins," said Cindy.

"Whew, that's a new development." The bartender seemed relieved. "Forget about paying for the drink. It's on the house."

Cindy was surprised. "No need for it."

"Listen, anyone that's helping out Paul is a friend of mine," he said. "His wife needs a hand, too."

The woman beside Cindy didn't seem to agree. "We women get what we deserve," she said under her breath.

"Kendra deserved this?" Cindy asked her, amazed.

The woman grabbed her drink and poured what was left of it down her throat. "I'm not saying Kendra in particular, I'm just saying a woman gets what she's willing to fight for."

Cindy was fascinated.

"Don't pay any attention to her," said the bartender. "She's had too much to drink—she rails against everything."

The woman next to Cindy put her glass down and asked for another. The bartender left to get it and she turned to Cindy.

"I had to ask for another to get rid of him. He's a terrific pain when he wants to be. Thinks he runs the island. Well, he doesn't, the only thing he runs is this bar. Paul was a big tipper, took good care of him. Paul's wife never came here though. The bartender never met her once."

"You knew Paul's wife well?" Cindy asked her.

"Not at all," said the woman, straightening out her skirt. "I knew Paul, though. He hung out here almost every night after work. Except when he was out of town." She looked at Cindy knowingly.

"Playing around?" said Cindy.

"I didn't say it, you did," said the woman.

"He came on to you?" Cindy wanted more.

"Never me. Never anyone I knew, either. Whenever I saw him he was just chatting it up with the girls. Paul loved to chat up the ladies and the guys as well. He needed attention. Tons of it. If you asked me, I could see this coming. He was a slippery kind of guy."

"How?"

"Honey, are you playing dumb or what? I thought you said you were a detective. Is this your act for getting me to spill the beans? Beautiful, sweet, innocent detective, looks like a lamb on the outside—but is really a tiger underneath."

Cindy respected how forthright she could be. "I'm new at this," she said, "I need to hear whatever you can tell me." The place was starting to get crowded and it was hard to hear over the din.

"I already told you" the woman said. "Paul was crafty, knew how to work the crowd, a few laughs here, a few smiles there. What for? I didn't buy it. I could see his mind ticking off all kinds of things. I mean if there's a wife waiting at home, what the hell was he doing hanging here?"

"Ever ask him that?"

"Come on. I know better. I come down here for the same thing he did. Company. Name is Andrea Bell, by the way. I own the spa two blocks down."

"Pleased to meet you," said Cindy.

The bartender returned. "She filling you in on the dirt in town?" he asked as he placed her drink in front of her.

"Come on, Perry," she said, "lighten up. You're a different guy since Paul died. Don't be so defensive."

"Nothing to do with being defensive," the bartender said, "just making sure that my friend gets his due respect."

"You get respect if you deserve it," said Andrea. "And it's as simple as that."

The bartender leaned in. "You think Paul didn't deserve it?"

"Who knows?" said Andrea.

The bartender turned to Cindy then. "This is a woman," he said, "who doesn't trust anyone. It comes from working in that spa for too many years. Hearing too many stories, from too many losers in town."

Cindy wondered if that would happen to her as well. Would she turn into another Andrea, doubting the motives of everyone?

"I'm a busy man," the bartender said then, "I can't stay here all night. You want to know more, come back and see me later." And he left.

"That's a hell of an invitation," Andrea said and kicked Cindy's foot under the bar. "You come back and you'll get more than conversation. You here alone?" she said.

"For tonight," said Cindy. "My partner, Mattheus, is out of town right now. Why?"

"Look, you got to know the lay of the land here. It's not so smart to prowl around on your own. Especially in a dress like that. Looks like you're out for a hot evening. But maybe you are? How do I know?"

"I'm not," Cindy said. "I'm out tonight to find out more about Paul and what happened to him."

"What do you want to know?" Andrea asked point-blank.

"Did he have a mistress? Was there someone he met here, or somewhere else?"

"I already told you," Andrea went on, "he chatted up lots of people."

"But was there one in particular?" Cindy sensed that Andrea knew more than she let on.

"And if there was," Andrea whispered, "what's in it for me?"

"You'd be helping out his wife, Kendra. The police are zeroed in on her."

"I couldn't care less about helping out Kendra."

Cindy was shocked. "You've something against her?"

"Not in particular, but I'm not the kind to help out wives in distress." She smiled broadly then. "Honest is honest. What else could be in it for me?"

"How much do you want?" asked Cindy.

Andrea smiled again. She had a tough charm. "Okay, you win. Buy the drinks I had tonight and we'll call it a deal."

Cindy took some cash out of her bag, as Andrea wrote something down on a paper cocktail napkin. She wrote it in a sprawling, slightly shaky handwriting. Cindy looked at the letters carefully. It was the name of a woman, Heather May. The writing was similar to the note she'd found—similar, but not a match.

"Who is she?" Cindy asked.

"You'll find out soon enough," she said, as she tossed her hair back and got up to leave. "It's been a pleasure meeting you."

"The pleasure's all mind," Cindy said.

Cindy folded the napkin and put it in her pocketbook. She wanted to get going. It was hot in here, the place was packed, and the noise of the band was too loud by now. Then, just as she was about to stand up, Cindy turned toward the doorway. Nojo was standing there, staring, blocking the door. Cindy stopped cold.

Then she walked toward the door, squeezing through the crowd. A few guys smiled at her as she wound her way through. When she got to the entrance, Nojo was blocking it.

"Hot out on the town?" he muttered under his breath, as Cindy stood in front of him.

Cindy pretended not to hear.

"Too bad your friend isn't here to watch over you now." Nojo spoke louder, chewing gum loudly.

Cindy tried to maneuver by.

"If there's one thing I hate," Nojo said, his voice louder, "it's snooty ladies who won't give you the time of day."

Cindy stopped in her tracks and stared him right in the eyes. "You're blocking my way," she said, her voice edgy and rough, a fierce anger suddenly rising in her.

Nojo wiped the grin off his face fast and moved to the side.

"See you later, doll," he drawled ominously, as Cindy slid past him out into the turbulent night.

CHAPTER 7

Mattheus wasn't due back until later that evening and Cindy was eager for him to return. She enjoyed going over plans for the day with him and filling him in on what had happened. Of course, she could have called him in St. Croix, but something stopped her. This was a new chapter for both of them and it had barely started. She didn't want to muddy the waters. She knew they needed distance between them and that it would give them both room to breathe. They also needed time to get to know each other. They'd jumped into an intense situation far too quickly, and above all, Cindy dreaded being suffocated or suffocating him.

When she woke up in the morning, she showered, dressed in a lime green, linen dress, and sat out on the patio of her hotel room. She'd have breakfast brought up, read the paper, and decide how to spend the day. Cindy put her legs up on a chair near the table and threw her head back, looking up at the sky. This work was certainly fascinating, if not tricky at times. She loved hunting down clues, meeting new people, following her gut instincts. So far, she'd put everything she'd gathered into a carved wooden box she'd found on the bureau of her room. Now she stuck Andrea's card in it and the napkin with the name of the woman she was to meet next. She also wanted to return to Kendra's and meet her daughter, Nell. Like separate pieces of a broken puzzle, they would all come together when the time was right.

There was a knock on her door and a waiter carried in breakfast on a tray. Cindy signed for it and thanked the waiter. Then she took her plate with her out onto the patio and ate slowly, enjoying the clear, salty morning air. The heat didn't start to come in until a little later, thick, muggy, humid weather at this time of year. It was lovely to take a few moments to enjoy the early morning breezes. She didn't have much time though. Clearly, her next move was to find the woman Andrea told her about, Heather May.

Cindy finished breakfast, picked up the phone, and asked for information. It could be just as simple as that. Heather May could be listed.

She wasn't.

Next Cindy called the police station and asked for Fred Brayton. After a few minutes he picked up the phone.

"Hi, this is Cindy Blaine."

There was silence for a second on the other side. "Oh yeah," he said finally. "I remember, sure. What's going on?" He sounded busy and official.

"I'm trying to find the address of a woman I want to talk to," Cindy said. "Can you give me a hand?"

"Who?" His interest perked up.

"Heather May," said Cindy.

He laughed.

Cindy was taken aback. "You know her?"

"Everybody knows her. We talked to her already, sweetheart. Who gave you her name?"

"The owner of Salon B," said Cindy, "Andrea."

He laughed harder. "Boy you sure get around town quick. Andrea's a character, all right. You been to the salon already?"

Cindy didn't like the tone in his voice. He spoke to her as if she were a child. "Not yet," she said, offended.

"That dame's a hoot. Where'd you meet her?" Brayton went on.

Enough was enough. Cindy wasn't going to join in bad-mouthing women. "I'd like Heather May's address and phone number if you have it," she said officially.

"That's a wild goose chase," Brayton answered. "She lives way at the edge of town, frizzy hair, always out on her porch, smoking dope. Fancies herself some kind of artist. She's not. Had a questionable connection with Paul too, if you asked me. Very peculiar. You can't believe a thing she says."

"Great," said Cindy, "I'd like to see her anyway."

"You're damn persistent for a woman, "Brayton said then.

Cindy shuddered and decided to have as little contact with the police as possible from now on. She didn't need them. She'd let Mattheus handle that.

"I'll run by her place for a little while," said Cindy. "Never know what I can pick up."

Brayton paused, grumbled, and acquiesced. "Do it your way, what do I care? Use your time however you like. I'm not the one paying for it." Then he gave her Heather May's address—42 Ravine Road. "It's down past the junction that leads to the pier on the left side of the island. Turn left there and keep going, until you can't go another minute. The house is there. A ramshackle place. I don't have her phone, don't know if she even has one."

Cindy hung up the phone. What was wrong with these guys? They lived in a time warp where women were treated like imbeciles. She could see clearly why women in trouble down here wanted a woman detective. At least Cindy had gotten Heather May's address. She decided to rent a car and drive down there herself to talk to her.

*

The trip down was tricky. The roads curved and wound up and down, along narrow edges and through hills lined with trees, wild bushes, sprawling vines. Lizards, frogs, and other little animals were everywhere, popping out at the most unexpected moments. The sun shone in Cindy's eyes most of the time as she drove.

This was probably a good trip to have taken with Mattheus, Cindy thought for a moment, and then quickly brushed the thought aside. She had to remember that Mattheus needed plenty of space. She'd felt a little pang when she thought about it, but brushed it away. This wasn't a relationship, it was a business partnership. They'd fill each other in when he got back into town. She'd chosen this job and had better grow strong enough to be able to handle it, learn to stand firmly on her own two feet. From the moment she'd met Clint years ago, she'd always felt taken care of. It had meant a lot to her then. Now things were different. Clint had been dead for a bunch of months, and she was in an equal partnership now.

She drove down a bumpy, unpaved road to the address she'd gotten for Heather May. This part of town was untouched, hidden and wild. Trees, brush, and wildlife of all kinds were tangled up in each other. Shafts of bright light shone through the trees and then disappeared suddenly in heavy shadows that lined the roads.

Cindy came to a small, wooden house with an open porch that wound around it. Beyond that, there was no road. Cindy got out of the car. A thick smell of leaves, pines, and moist soil wafted up. This had to be Heather May's place. She walked closer, feeling like an intruder, trying not to make a sound.

To Cindy's surprise the sound of chimes rang out as she got closer to the entrance. They were hanging along the edge of the porch, ready to warn whoever was inside that someone was approaching. Just as Cindy expected, the front door opened then, and a woman in her mid-forties came out. She had on a long cotton skirt and skimpy T-shirt. Her long, golden, frizzy hair framed a pretty face. She stared at Cindy, uncomprehending.

"I'm Cindy Blaine," Cindy announced, before she took another step. The last thing she wanted to do in the world was frighten this woman, who already seemed startled and alone.

"Who?" the woman asked softly, confused.

"Andrea gave me your name," Cindy said then.

The woman curled her forehead, thinking. "From Salon B?" she asked finally.

Cindy nodded.

"Okay," she said then, smiling slightly, "come on up."

Cindy took small steps carefully as she approached her, aware that Heather May was examining her from head to toe.

"I'm Heather May," the woman said finally, in a soft tone.

Cindy was relieved that she'd passed inspection and Heather was talking to her.

"Sit down out here on the porch," said Heather. "I'll go in and get you some lemonade."

"There's no need for lemonade," said Cindy, not wanting to put her to any trouble.

"Of course there is," said Heather. "It's refreshing in the afternoon, especially before the heavy clouds come. And they come more often these days, just before the hurricane season." Then she wiped her hands along the sides of her skirt, turned, and walked back in.

The porch had a few wicker chairs and an old, red, leather glider that was ripped here and there. Cindy wanted to sit on the glider, but she chose a wicker chair with plump tropical cushions on it.

In a few minutes, Heather came out, carrying lemonade glasses with a slice of lime and cherry in them. She offered one to Cindy, staring straight into her eyes. Then she laughed.

"Two days ago, Marshmallow told me someone unexpected would be arriving. I didn't really believe what he said. I never do. And he's almost never wrong."

Cindy smiled. "Who's Marshmallow?"

"He reads the stars, feels the tides, knows when the earth is turning."

Despite her wild, frizzy hair Heather had a strange beauty that pulled you in.

"Thanks for having me here," Cindy said then, raising the lemonade to her lips. It was delicious and hit the spot.

"You've come about Paul?" Heather asked then, drinking her lemonade along with Cindy, eyes half closed.

"How did you know?" asked Cindy, startled.

"No other reason Andrea would have sent you. She and I spent hours together after he died, going over every last detail. It was a terrible shock to everyone."

"I can imagine," said Cindy.

Heather gazed at her calmly. "Yes, you can," she said. "You've been there. I feel it, you understand."

Cindy breathed more easily. She and Heather had an odd kinship; they understood one another, appreciated what each had been through.

"How long did you know Paul?" Cindy asked carefully.

"It was not that I knew him," Heather said quietly, "it was that he was my whole life. Our love affair lasted for about three years. It kept both of us going. Can you understand that?"

Cindy nodded. "Yes, of course," she said.

"I believe you. I see that you've suffered," Heather said. "Actually, you can't believe a person or trust them unless they've suffered terribly."

Her voice grew louder, like music, thought Cindy.

"If we hadn't been together when we were, Paul could not have gone on," Heather said. "Our relationship filled a deep need of his that nothing else ever could."

Cindy wondered for a moment how true that was. She resisted the impulse to look around the place Heather lived in and wonder why Paul hadn't fixed it up for her.

Heather laughed then, as if reading Cindy's mind. "I like my place just as it is. I'm different from the others. I didn't want his money. That's why he needed me."

Cindy smiled then. "I understand," she said.

"Paul was an incredibly hungry man," Heather said softly, leaning toward Cindy. She seemed to get pleasure talking about him. "I'm not saying I was all he needed, but I was an important part. Very important."

"Were you in a relationship when he was killed?" Cindy asked softly.

"Are you a detective or something?" Heather asked then.

Cindy nodded slowly.

"Really?" said Heather, giggling with delight. "It becomes you. This is your right work. You're soft and gentle. People sense it. You'll find out everything you need this way. Don't give it up."

"I don't plan to give it up," said Cindy.

"You might though," said Heather. "You're tangling with a vicious world. It might not look that way at first, but under the smiles and flowers, this place is a terrifying jungle."

Cindy breathed deeply.

"The human heart is a jungle," Heather went on. "You don't know how much yet, but you'll soon find out." Then she finished the rest of her lemonade.

Cindy drank along with her and they both put their glasses down at the same moment.

"I believe you've been sent to me to encourage you. Do you do this work alone?" Heather asked, curious.

"I have a partner," said Cindy.

"A guy?"

"Yes, another detective."

Heather smiled. "He's probably madly in love with you, pretending to be all business."

"Not at all," said Cindy, flinching. It wasn't like that and she didn't want it to be.

"Of course he is, that's how guys are."

Cindy smiled and felt a pang of pain. "Not in this case. We're both involved in the work," she said. "That's it."

"That's what they all say," said Heather.

"My husband was killed just a few months ago," Cindy couldn't help saying. "On our honeymoon."

Heather's mouth dropped open. "That's horrible."

Cindy wasn't exactly sure why she'd told her that. Maybe she just wanted to preserve Clint's memory and give him respect.

"You loved him tremendously, you adored him," Heather May breathed softly.

"I did," said Cindy.

"That's why you're here now, tracking down crimes. Oh my dear, I'm honored to meet you."

Cindy was surprised by her reaction. "Thank you."

"Ask me anything you want. I'll be happy to tell you."

"Well, I need to know where you were the day Paul was killed."

Heather smiled. She was too smart not to realize what Cindy was asking. "You're wondering about my alibi?" she said. "I gave it to the police already. It checked out, thank God, because I'm often here alone. That particular afternoon there was a design show down at the museum. I was part of the planning committee, so I went. A lot of people from town were there, furniture designers, painters, architects. We have it once a year. It attracts lots of tourists. In fact, Kendra usually came as well. She woke up that morning, feeling ill."

Cindy enjoyed speaking with Heather, but realized that there was still an important question she hadn't answered. "Were you and Paul still a couple when he was killed?" Cindy asked again softly.

"No, we weren't," said Heather, resigned to being questioned. "It was over for a couple of years by then."

"How come?"

Heather looked away, out into the woods that surrounded her small home. It was clear she hadn't come to terms with it yet.

"Lots of reasons?" Cindy prodded her.

"No," said Heather, "just one. One reason that ended it suddenly."

The sound of a lone macaw pierced the afternoon.

"Those birds always act up before the hurricanes come. We have a week or two to get ready," Heather said. "Not long now. You can feel the winds stirring in your veins in the early morning down here."

"Are you with someone else now?" Cindy couldn't let go.

"I'll never be with someone else again," Heather said, suddenly stern, staring at Cindy, her eyes full of pain.

"I'm sorry," said Cindy.

"Don't be," said Heather. "What Paul and I had was worth it. The years we had together will hold me a whole lifetime."

Cindy was moved. She wondered if she felt that way about Clint. Could the memory of the time they had together last her a lifetime and beyond? She didn't think so. Already, she felt the loneliness tug at her.

Cindy didn't want to intrude, but she had to know more. "Did Paul break it off?"

"No, I did," said Heather.

Cindy was surprised. "Can you tell me why?"

"I could if I wanted, but I don't want to," Heather said. "Actually, I'll do better than tell you. I'll give you the address of someone to see. Go there and see her. And you'll find out everything you need to know.

Heather grabbed some paper that was lying on a small table and quickly wrote a name and address on it. Then she handed it to Cindy.

Cindy inspected the paper carefully. Her handwriting was bold, fierce, unstoppable. It took Cindy back. All the lines for the future sloped upward, filled with confidence and promise. It didn't fit with the story she told.

"This is powerful handwriting, "said Cindy.

Heather lifted her head, proudly.

"It shows that you're not afraid of anything."

"I'm not," said Heather in a deeper tone. "I'm not alone because I'm afraid. I'm alone because I refuse to have another broken heart. These things can destroy you."

"How well I know," said Cindy.

"Then keep your eyes wide open," said Heather. "It's easier than you think to let yourself get ripped apart."

CHAPTER 8

Mattheus couldn't get Roomey Burke out of his mind all during the flight home. The guy had a compelling way that got under your skin. The fact that he considered himself part of Paul and Kendra's family interested Mattheus tremendously. The guy had influence over Kendra. Maybe she didn't need the two million from the insurance, but he could sure use some of it. First thing back, Mattheus would check his alibi. It wasn't enough to find out whether or not Roomey was at the show; he'd have to find out how long he'd actually stayed. Mattheus had also gotten the name of the guy in the high-stakes poker game, Silbert Hours, who was indebted to Paul. As soon as he checked out Roomey's alibi, he'd find out about him.

The plane landed easily and Mattheus took a quick cab back to the hotel. It was good getting away, but he was glad to be back, too. As the cab pulled up to the hotel, he realized he hadn't let Cindy know what time he'd be returning. He got out of the cab and suddenly felt curious about where she was now and what she'd been up to.

Mattheus walked into the lobby, half expecting her to be sitting there, waiting for him. She wasn't. He went up to the front desk and asked them to ring her room. As he took the phone his palms felt a little sweaty. This new arrangement between them would take some getting used to. He'd spent the last three years on the police force dealing with guys and set schedules. The phone rang in her room several times. No one picked up. Mattheus looked at the phone, disconcerted.

"Happen to see Cindy Blaine this morning?" he asked the guy at the desk.

"Who?" The guy didn't recognize the name.

"Beautiful blonde woman in her thirties, from the states."

The guy at the desk raised his eyes. "Oh, of course," he said, "how can you miss her? I think the past day or two she had breakfast on the patio restaurant over there." He pointed to one of the hotel restaurants. "She's expecting you?"

The question took Mattheus back. Even though he'd told her generally when he'd be back, he'd been purposely vague. There was no reason for her to be expecting him, to be hanging around, waiting. That was a mistake on his part, Mattheus realized instantly. They needed to fill each other in and make plans about who would do what next.

Disconcerted, Mattheus walked toward the restaurant the guy had pointed out. It was only 9:30 in the morning. He hoped, by luck, she'd still be there.

The restaurant was down at the end of the lobby, overlooking a large garden, filled with wildflowers, plants, little iguanas, and island birds chirping all day long. To Mattheus' delight, the minute he walked in, he saw Cindy seated at a front table, drinking coffee and reading the local paper. His heart stopped a second, and he held back. She looked beautiful sitting there in the sunlight, dressed in a soft, blue and green printed cotton dress. She seemed strangely comfortable and at ease, as if she fit right into the lush tropical landscape.

Mattheus walked over and she suddenly looked up, startled.

"My goodness," said Cindy, "I had no idea you'd returned."

Mattheus pulled out a chair for himself at the table. "Mind if I join you?"

Cindy smiled. She was confident and more than a little suntanned.

"Of course, join me," she said.

Mattheus sat down. He'd had breakfast on the plane, but could easily eat more now. The beautiful weather, trees, and fresh air constantly sparked his appetite. He ordered scrambled eggs and coffee, as the waiter refilled Cindy's coffee cup.

"Tell me about your trip," she started, putting the paper down. "Useful?"

"Very," said Mattheus. "Checked the records at the casinos—Paul played in a high-stakes poker game and a guy in the game was badly indebted to him. A great reason to take him out. I'm going to check into hm. Beyond that, I met a gambling buddy of his, Roomey Burke. Strange character who said Kendra talked to him a lot. Told him she was lonely toward the end of their marriage."

Cindy raised her eyebrows slightly, as if that wasn't such a surprise. "Not so unusual," she said softly.

Mattheus agreed. "True, except that it's interesting to notice that Kendra spoke about it to him."

Cindy nodded. "Or so he says."

Mattheus smiled. Cindy was getting tougher by the day, not taking anything at face value. "Okay," said Mattheus, "but why would he make it up? What's in it for him?"

"Sometimes a guy enjoys feeling that he holds a special place in a woman's life," she said, "even when he doesn't. Guys blow things up in their mind. It can make them feel important."

Mattheus didn't like that. This was a part of Cindy he hadn't yet seen. "You sound bitter," he said.

"Not at all. Just realistic. There's lots of characters here, floating on the fringes. Who knows what they had to do with the murder? I don't want to jump to conclusions, just keep my mind open."

Mattheus' breakfast came and he ate it quickly.

"You're starving," said Cindy, "didn't you eat on the plane?"

"I did," said Mattheus, wolfing it down.

Cindy suddenly looked concerned about him and extended her hand for a moment. Then she quickly took it back. "I'd like to meet this Roomey Burke," she said.

"You will," said Mattheus, between mouthfuls. "What about you? Who did you find?" It was great being with her, but it also made him nervous.

"I had a great two days," said Cindy. "Met a couple of fascinating women. One owns the spa in town, Salon B. She gave me the name of another woman, Heather May, who claims she had a romance with Paul for about three years. Said it was over for a long time before the murder happened, though."

Mattheus put his fork down, startled and impressed. "That's important information. The guy had a mistress—whew. The police didn't mention anything about it. Are you sure she's not fantasizing?"

"I wondered about that myself at first," said Cindy, "but the more we talked the more solid her story seemed. She said their time together was incredible, gave him something he never had anywhere else."

Mattheus smiled at that. "Guess women like to think that, as well."

"Heather May wasn't angry with him either, seemed to be suffering because of his death."

"So, the guy played around," mused Mattheus. "Not so good for Kendra. It could be more fuel for her motive to get rid of him."

"Or, it could implicate the mistress," said Cindy.

"Could," said Mattheus, "but that's farfetched if the relationship was over. Why would she want to get rid of him now? This goes more to Paul's character. A cheater lies. Usually they're good at it. Especially if they've had a long relationship on the side.

For all we know this guy could have gotten caught in a web of lies that finally drove someone crazy. Crazy enough to kill him for it."

Cindy was fascinated listening to Mattheus spin a web, constructing a theory from nothing much. "You're good at this." She smiled.

Mattheus smiled back. "So, tell me more," he said. "How did you meet the gal who owns the spa?"

"Went to the bar where Paul was a regular."

At that Mattheus looked up at her keenly. "At night? Alone?"

"Sure," said Cindy.

"You must have created quite a stir." Mattheus felt uneasy.

"Just business," Cindy said. "It was crowded and noisy. I have the woman's card. Her name is Andrea. She seems to know what's going on in town."

"Talk to any guys?" he asked rather casually.

Cindy smiled. "A couple, here and there. Why?"

Mattheus shrugged and put his fork down.

"There was one guy who troubled me though," Cindy said, suddenly uneasy. "That cop at the station, Nojo, was there. He kept staring at me, was rude, threatening."

Mattheus' jaw clenched. He felt agitated by the story.

"I don't recommend you go to those places alone," he said in a strained tone. "Wait for me to go with you. That's what I'm here for." The thought of her drifting around alone in these bars made his skin crawl.

"Other than Nojo, I had a good time. It was useful, meeting Andrea."

Let's make a plan right now," Mattheus said. He wanted to set up a structure between them that would make them both comfortable, that would work. "For starters, I'll handle the bars and night spots."

Cindy put her coffee cup down. "If I need to go there, you can come with me, too," she acquiesced. "More importantly, though, you handle the cops. I'll speak to the women, friends, and family."

"Good," said Mattheus. "l will check out Roomey's alibi today, contact the poker player, and also get in touch with the police about the cases Paul lost. I'm going to the police station first thing."

"Great," said Cindy. "I can't shake the feeling that someone Paul defended could be involved in this. How about you?"

"Anything's possible," said Mattheus. "That's what's so fascinating about our work. What are your next steps?"

"Before I go to see the woman Heather May suggested, I want to meet the main players in the case, particularly Kendra's daughter,

Nell. Kendra mentioned that she'd be home from school this morning. How about running over there with me for an hour, then we'll go our separate ways."

"Sounds good to me," said Mattheus. "After that, I also think we should take some time to visit Paul's office, meet some colleagues, look around. That'll give us both a fuller backdrop of his life."

"Great," said Cindy. "I want to be completely prepared before I go see that woman. Heather May told me that when I met her, I'd find out all I needed to know."

Mattheus pulled back at that one. It was a red light signal. "That's quite a claim," he said. "Don't get your hopes up too high. When people promise me the moon, I usually take a few steps back."

Cindy looked sad suddenly and Mattheus wondered why.

"Sounds like you're afraid to trust," she said.

"I trust when trust is earned," he said. "It takes time. That's smart."

"I trusted Heather May," said Cindy.

"I'm not sure why," said Mattheus. "It sounds to me like Heather May has her own agenda, her own reality."

"I liked her," said Cindy.

"Liking her and believing her are two different things," Mattheus said. "Could be she's sending you on a wild goose chase. Some people enjoy creating confusion. Others get a payoff by sending you in the wrong direction. The worst thing is to expect one lead to solve all your problems. That clouds your vision, creates disappointment. Takes you off your game."

If Mattheus knew anything, it was how to stay on his game. Cindy enjoyed listening to his observations, absorbing what he'd learned.

"You're right," said Cindy. "Heather May seems to live on the edge. She could just be having an island fantasy. I've got to find out more about her, as well."

"Okay," said Mattheus. "First we'll check in on Nell. Before we do, I want the address of the woman you're going to interview later, in case you need cover."

Cindy gave him the address reluctantly. "I won't need cover," she said.

Mattheus didn't like that. "You never know," he said. "I should know where you are at all times."

"Should I know where you are as well?" Cindy asked, playfully.

Mattheus grimaced. "You plan to cover me in case of danger?" he asked offhandedly.

"I'd contact the police immediately," said Cindy.

The idea amused him. "Let's play it one step at a time," he answered simply, and pulled his chair out to go. Cindy didn't seem eager to go anywhere, though, just sat there looking at him and then out at the gardens spread out before her. The flowers were waving slightly in the wind that was beginning to blow up. Mattheus had a sudden urge to sit back down with her, take some time. But he could feel the winds changing and realized the storms weren't far behind. There was a lot to be done before then.

"Come on, let's get going," he said. "There's a lot to be covered. We don't have time for just looking at the sky."

Cindy got up. "I'm going to the ladies' room for a second, and then we can be on our way," she said.

*

Mattheus sat back down and watched her walk to the ladies' room. She had an easy grace as she moved, like a tree swaying in the breeze. He was amazed at how good it had been to sit there with her after returning from St. Croix. He'd expected all kinds of repercussions about his not being in touch. They didn't come. He was also surprised how relieved he felt to be doing his part of the investigation alone. He had no intention of letting her know where he'd be every minute. It wasn't that she didn't have a right to know, it was that it made him feel too closed in. He needed space and privacy, always had, even during his marriage. He flinched now as he thought of those years married to Shelly. She'd complained all the time about not knowing where he was, or when exactly he was returning. He'd always returned, though, been happy to see her, and taken good care of her. Except on that fatal afternoon. Mattheus tried to wipe it out of his mind again. Now that was one time he should have been closer. One time that changed everyone's life.

CHAPTER 9

Before they jumped into the cab Cindy called Kendra and said they'd be coming for an hour or so. They wanted to talk to Nell. Kendra said she didn't much see the point in that, but it was as good a time as any to do so. Nell was home for the day, up in her room.

They got the cab in front of the hotel, and as they rode to Kendra's, Cindy looked out the window. She'd known Mattheus was coming back to St. Thomas that day, but hadn't expected him to show up at breakfast like that. Since they'd arrived on the island, Mattheus had shown so many different sides to him, she didn't know what to expect next. Back on Grenada he felt like a rock to her, constant, caring, dependable. Now he seemed skittish at times, even eager to get away from her. She couldn't help compare him to Clint, who had been fully available when he was around. Cindy'd never felt he wanted to run away. The sense that Mattheus was unsettled made her feel insecure. Of course, their company didn't have to last forever. If it didn't work out, Cindy could always go home.

When Cindy and Mattheus arrived and rang the doorbell, Kendra opened the door immediately. She wore beige slacks and a linen shirt, with a matching necklace and bracelet. Her long hair was tied back from her face. It struck Cindy as odd that a woman whose husband had been murdered such a short time ago would be so perfectly groomed.

"Come in," said Kendra somewhat officially.

Cindy and Mattheus came in and looked around for Nell.

"Nell's in her room," said Kendra. "She's studying. The kids have off from school for a few days for exams. The police spoke to her quite a bit in the beginning. I don't know what she can possibly add now."

"We just wanted to meet the whole family," said Cindy. "It won't take long."

Kendra sighed. "It all adds up, though. Half an hour here, an hour there."

It sounded as if she resented their being there. "We want to do a thorough job," said Cindy.

Kendra interrupted, "Thorough or not is one thing. Finding the killer is something else. How in the world can Nell lead you to that?"

"You never know what one offhanded comment leads to," said Mattheus, "especially from someone close to the victim."

"Do what you have to," said Kendra. "Nell," she called loudly then, her voice bouncing off the high walls. "Come downstairs."

No answer.

"She's probably deep on her Facebook page." Kendra smirked. "That's about all these kids study these days, who's saying what to who? Nell—" Her voice rose with a sharp timbre.

Cindy heard a door open upstairs. She looked up and saw a young, tall, slender woman come down. She had long, dark hair, a sculpted face, and extremely intense eyes.

When the young woman got down the stairs, she paid no attention to her mother, but came right over to Cindy and said, "Hello, I'm Nell."

"Glad to meet you, Nell," said Cindy.

"I'm glad to see you finally managed to extricate yourself and come downstairs," Kendra quipped. "Whenever she's home, Nell practically lives in her room these days. She never has a second to spend with me."

"This has been a horrible strain on my mother," Nell said to Cindy abruptly. "You have to help the authorities realize that she's had absolutely nothing to do with this crime."

Kendra looked at her oddly. "I've told them that already," she said. "That's why they're here. I believe they'll help."

Cindy looked over at Nell, who suddenly turned sullen. "Nothing I say makes any difference," she said.

"We'd love to hear more from you, Nell," Cindy said, breaking into the thick tension that had formed. "Let's sit down a moment."

Nell shot her mother a quick look and then went with Cindy and Mattheus to the couch. Kendra started to join them as well.

"We'd like to talk to Nell alone," said Mattheus.

Kendra was offended. "Why?"

"People can talk more easily when they're alone," he said. "It won't take very long."

"This is not a matter of time," said Kendra. "What could Nell possibly say that I can't hear? You're working for me, after all."

Nell looked down at the floor.

"Would you like me to join you?" Kendra asked Nell pointedly.

Nell did not respond.

"It's better this way," Cindy said gently.

"Have it your way," said Kendra, irritated, and stalked out of the room.

When she left Nell took a deep breath. "My mother has moods, she always had. And now it's particularly tough for her."

"You don't get along so well?" asked Cindy.

"Up and down. She's hard to take. I was closer to my father."

"I'm sorry," said Cindy. "You must miss him very much."

Nell's eyes suddenly closed.

"Is there anything at all you can tell us?" Cindy asked in as gentle a voice as she could. Nell was odd and interesting. At moments she was extremely alert, and then at other moments, remote, as if a cloud had descended upon her.

"I have no idea who killed my father, "said Nell, finally, opening her eyes slightly. Her face flushed as she spoke. Just saying those words was painful for her. "I don't even want to know who did it. I want to wake up and find out it was all a bad dream."

"It wasn't a dream," said Cindy.

"How do you know?" said Nell. "People can live their whole lives and then something happens and their whole life turns into a dream."

"That's what happened to you?" asked Mattheus.

"None of it's real," said Nell.

Cindy and Mattheus looked at each other. Cindy didn't want to push too hard. This was so new and fresh for Nell, it would take months for her to make sense of it. And clearly, she didn't have the kind of relationship with her mother that would support her through the process. Yet, oddly enough, she didn't seem so alone. There was a strange strength about her.

"I'm more like my dad," Nell said then from out of nowhere. "We understood each other very well."

"How wonderful that you had that," said Cindy.

"He didn't let anything knock him down." Her eyes opened wider and she seemed to get strength just thinking about him. "Once he said, Nell, no matter what the world dishes out, remember one thing, honey. You can always find a way out of a tough spot. There's always another street to walk down, there's always an answer waiting."

Mattheus seemed impressed. "Quite a guy," he said.

Nell's face lit up briefly. "He was a great guy—he was different," she said.

"It must have been a powerful force that took him down," said Mattheus.

Nell recoiled. "I don't know what happened." She shook her head.

Cindy got up from the couch and walked over to her. It was enough. She didn't want Mattheus crashing through Nell's defenses all at once. She needed them now.

"In a little while the storm season's starting," Nell went on, out of nowhere.

"And?" asked Cindy.

"All the tourists leave the island. Only the hard-core remain. We board up our homes and get ready to wait out the storm inside. My dad always loved hurricane season. He and I boarded up the house together, year after year."

"Who's going to board it up this year?" asked Mattheus.

"No one," said Nell, smiling oddly. "Maybe this year the storm will just tear the whole house apart."

*

"There was no reason to grill her like that," said Cindy, when she and Mattheus had left the house. "You were too tough on her."

"I had to be," said Mattheus. "When they're rattled they say things they wouldn't otherwise say. Things just come out."

"What about her?" said Cindy. "She's a kid who's lost her dad."

"I'm sorry for her," said Mattheus, "but I don't forget what I'm here to do. I wasn't hired to be a therapist. Neither were you. We have a big job to do and not much time to do it. Beyond all that, there's a murderer on the loose. You never know when they'll strike again, or who?"

The way he said it gave Cindy a chill. She hadn't taken in the fact that right among them, close by possibly, the murderer could be lurking, waiting to pounce.

"You're right," she said to Mattheus then. "Right and wrong at the same time."

He looked at her quizzically.

"We've got to find the killer, but we've got to take care of the others too. Paul wasn't the only victim. His whole family was as well."

"Point well taken," said Mattheus, as he looked at Cindy, his eyes filled with respect. "That's why it's good to have both a male and female on the case. Nothing gets overlooked."

"I'm going to spend some more time here with Kendra," Cindy said.

“Great,” said Mattheus. “In the meantime, I’ll run over to the police station and look up some information I need. Then we can meet up and take a look at Paul’s office, in about an hour. Okay?”

“Okay,” said Cindy. Everything was okay and not okay. Not only was she finding out more about the case, but also about Mattheus. There were definitely moments when he scared her. Who had she really ended up here with?

CHAPTER 10

Before Mattheus went to the police station, he called some of his buddies back on the force in Grenada, to check in and let them know what was going on. They were thrilled to hear from him, as usual, and suggested he check out Roomey's alibi before taking another step. Guys who hung around casinos needed to be vetted right away. Mattheus agreed. And when was he coming back to Grenada? they wanted to know. It wasn't the same place without him.

The calls to the guys back home gave Mattheus energy, boosted his spirits and resolve. They'd become like a little family, and Mattheus missed having them around. But he also enjoyed the adventure of starting his own enterprise. And he enjoyed doing it with Cindy, who surprised him over and over with her keen intelligence and strength.

After he hung up he headed to the police station, to use the computers there to check on Roomey further. There was no one at the back desk yet, and he had his pick of places to work at. He quickly opened a computer and brought up what he could find on Roomey. The more he read, the more impressed he was. Not only did everything about him seem legit, but he was a well-respected architect, with big clients to his name. Easy to see why the guy could afford to lose at high-stakes poker.

Then Mattheus dug up the name of the organizer of the design show Roomey said he was at to give him a call and find out exactly when Roomey arrived, and how long he stayed.

Roomey's alibi checked out completely. Not only was he at the show, he got there early and stayed until it closed. Something he did every year, apparently. After it was over, he went out with a few people for a light dinner. He went with a group of old-timers who came to the show year after year. Some of the people at the dinner included Andrea from Salon B, a couple of guys who sponsored the program, and Heather May. Mattheus found it interesting to see her name pop up again. But of course, this was a relatively small island and the people who lived here had to know each other. He wondered briefly what kind of relationship Roomey had with Heather, and made a note to ask Cindy to explore it. Mattheus also wanted to see Roomey again, catch a drink with him, find out more about Kendra and about Paul.

Okay, thought Mattheus, one down and another to go. He now wanted to check out the guy in the high-stakes poker game. Just as he was about to go back into the computer, the door to the station opened and Brayton came in and immediately spotted Mattheus in the rear.

"Hey, what you doing back there?" Brayton hollered, as he came over to join Mattheus.

"Checking out Roomey and some other guys."

"You don't let up, do you?" Brayton said, approvingly. "Too bad we don't have you on our force down here."

Mattheus grinned. It felt good having the team around him, surrounded by guys who valued him. Mattheus was one of a twin, and his brother had been the star in everything, got all the attention, growing up.

"No reason to bother checking out Roomey," Brayton said as he sat down. "Could have told you about him before you started to look. He's an old-timer on the island. There's no reason to suspect him of anything. Roomey and Paul had been friends for years."

"Was there was ever anything floating around about Roomey's relationship with Kendra?" Mattheus asked.

Brayton laughed. "Roomey's not exactly a ladies' man. The furthest thing from it. The guy keeps to himself around the ladies. They don't like him much, and he doesn't really take to them."

"Did he take to Kendra?" Mattheus pushed on.

"What are you dreaming up?" Brayton looked at Mattheus as though he were a little crazy. "We've got enough on Kendra, we don't need this. When you get desperate for clues you can fish in places where nothing bites," he said. "Doesn't do any good to make up crazy stories. In fact, it's downright dangerous."

"You're right," Mattheus agreed. Then he told him about the high-stakes poker game Paul had been involved in.

Brayton was taken aback. "Now, that's something to chew on. Don't know how we didn't hear about that. Find the guy who was indebted to Paul and bring him in to talk."

Mattheus had his name; it would be an easy matter to check him out right away.

"What else you got?" asked Brayton.

"That's it for now," said Mattheus. "More on the way." He was looking forward to hearing what Cindy would bring him next as well. Mattheus realized how much he trusted her ability to tune into unexpected clues and run into people who were able to steer them where nobody else had thought to go.

"Well, it's great to have you around," said Brayton, scraping his chair back on the floor to get up. "Feel free to use anything you need here to help, and let me know if there's anything I can do."

"Appreciate that," said Mattheus, really meaning it.

Brayton went back to his office, and Mattheus dove back into the computer, searching for information on Silbert Hours, the guy in the poker game. His photo came up right away, a sleazy-looking fellow with long, curly hair, wearing a few gold chains. His records said he owned a massage parlor on the south side of town. Mattheus wondered if it had anything to do with Andrea, and Salon B. He read further and saw that Silbert's place was far away. The guy looked so scraggly Mattheus wondered where he got his money from. His massage place was probably a front for something, Mattheus thought. Nothing else much came up about him. He had no police record, no bankruptcies. Mattheus quickly wrote down his address and the phone number of the parlor, and planned to pay him a visit there.

Just as he was writing down the information, Mattheus felt someone come and stand behind him, looking over his shoulder. Mattheus turned and looked up. It was Nojo.

"What's that address you're writing down?" asked Nojo.

"A guy named Silbert Hours."

Nojo grinned. "Damned if you don't get the craziest information. What in hell has this case got to do with him?"

"You know the guy?" Mattheus was surprised.

"Everybody knows Silbert Hours," said Nojo. "A pathetic loser if ever there was one."

"He runs a massage parlor?" said Mattheus.

Nojo laughed out loud. "Yeah, yeah, tell me another. "He sells the ladies—for a fistful of dough."

Mattheus listened. It made sense to him.

"And he gets a big piece of the pie. That massage parlor rakes in more than you can imagine."

That explained where this guy got his money for the high-stakes game.

"I want to find out where he was when Paul was killed," Mattheus said.

"Oh brother," Nojo snorted. "Silbert Hours never goes out in the daylight. It hurts his eyes. You want to find out where he was that day? You'll have to ask the ladies and their customers."

"You're sure about this?" asked Mattheus.

"Positive."

"I'm still going to check it out."

"Enjoy yourself," said Nojo. "It's as good an excuse as any to get a freebie." And he laughed and laughed so hard that Mattheus had to get up and walk away.

"And just remember," Nojo yelled after him, "that nothing on this island's free! There's a price to pay for everything! Those ladies there are vicious. They'll rip your heart in two." Then he laughed and laughed again so hard that it sounded like an old caw had gotten trapped in the rafters of the house, and was struggling to get free.

CHAPTER 11

Cindy and Mattheus met up and decided to drop in at Paul's old office unannounced. It was in a fairly modern, mid-sized, air-conditioned building on the third floor. On the door it said Robbins and Jeffries, Criminal Defense Attorneys. They opened the door, walked in, and were greeted by the receptionist, as if everything were normal, and it was just another day.

"Can I help you?" She smiled prettily.

"Private investigators," Mattheus said. "We're investigating the murder of Paul Robbins and would like to look around."

The smile on her face quickly vanished. "I'm sorry," she said, startled, and stood up quickly. "Mr. Jeffries is out right now and I don't have the authority to let you into his office."

Mattheus pulled out his old police identification to show her.

Nervous, she stepped back.

"We're not going to do anything more than look around," said Mattheus. "Mr. Robbins' wife, Kendra, has hired us to help out."

The receptionist's eyes, confused and helpless, flitted to Cindy.

"It's perfectly all right," Cindy said soothingly. "We'll be in and out in a little while."

That seemed to calm her down.

"Okay," she said suddenly, "but just for a little while. Mr. Jeffries is on edge about everything since this happened."

"It's understandable," Cindy said.

"He goes out for coffee breaks all the time, and leaves earlier than he ever did."

"It had to be a tremendous shock," said Cindy.

"Tremendous," she said, finally coming out from behind her desk. "My name is Peggy."

"Nice to meet you." Cindy extended her hand.

Peggy was young, slim, and wore a gray skirt and pale, rose-colored blouse that hung over the edges.

"I'll open Mr. Robbins' office for you," she said.

"I'm sure the police have already been through it," said Mattheus.

"Just once," she answered, "and briefly. That also bothered Mr. Jeffries that the police didn't spend more time in the office, seeing what they could find. I heard Mr. Jeffries telling someone that the police never thought the answers were here."

Cindy and Mattheus followed her down a hallway to a door on the right. She took the key she'd brought with her and unlocked the door.

Paul's office was a large room, overlooking a busy square where people were walking, shops were open for business, and cars driving here and there. The windows were shut tight and the air conditioning turned up high. It was so cold Cindy got a chill when she walked inside.

"He loved this office," Peggy said sadly. "I haven't been in it since Mr. Jeffries locked down. He was worried that something would be messed with or stolen."

A large wooden desk stood in the middle of the room, with a comfortable leather chair behind it and two smaller chairs in front. The side of the room had filing cabinets, a small sofa, and old wooden bookcases that were filled from top to bottom. Other than that, the walls were covered with large photos of Kendra and Nell.

Cindy looked at the photos, touched. "He must have really loved his family," she said.

"Very much," said Peggy. "Kendra called him all the time. So did his daughter. No matter what he was doing, he always stopped and took their calls."

Cindy felt sad to hear that. She could only imagine what a loss it must be for both of them.

"Mr. Robbins always said to me, Peggy, remember one thing, family is first."

Cindy remembered that Paul had trouble with his original family back home. That's why Kendra and Nell must have meant so much.

"What else did he tell you?" Mattheus asked, walking around, going to the front of his desk, opening the drawers, poking around.

"About what?" Peggy asked, confused.

"About himself, about life?"

"Not much," she finally said. "He told me to always be on time to work." She smiled a little. "He hated it when people were late. And he said to be polite to everyone who came in, including the worst-looking ones. He told me over and over that everyone deserves a chance."

"But he didn't get it himself, did he?" said Mattheus.

Cindy was startled by the edge in Mattheus' tone.

"In fact, it could have been one of these criminals that finally did him in?" Mattheus threw a side glance at Peggy.

Peggy jumped back. Mattheus seemed to be taking pleasure in purposely jarring her.

"It could have been anyone," Peggy said quietly. "I have no idea. I don't like thinking about it. I wouldn't be able to come in to work here if I did."

Cindy wanted to step in between Peggy and Mattheus, but something in his eyes told her to back away. He was doing this for a reason.

"Was there someone who came in recently that you felt funny about?" Mattheus said.

Peggy's eyes clouded over. "I didn't pay much attention to the clients," she said. "I didn't feel comfortable with most of them."

"Mr. Robbins did though?"

"He loved them." She looked Mattheus straight in the eye then. "I used to hear him talking to them in the waiting room and also on the phone. He made them feel confident and protected. Seemed he always wanted to get them the best deal."

This was hard for Peggy and Cindy could see it. But just then, the door to Paul's office flew open and a tall, thin, agitated man walked in.

"What's going on here?"

"It's the police," said Peggy nervously. "They're investigating the case."

"Jeffries here." He turned toward Mattheus. "Who sent you to our place?"

"Private investigators," said Mattheus. "We've been hired by Mrs. Robbins."

Jeffries cleared his throat. "I heard about that," he said. "She's desperate to clear her name."

"We're following any leads we can get now." Mattheus looked him straight in the eye.

"Believe me, I've been over this a million times," Jeffries said hastily. "Been through his drawers myself, looking for something. There's nothing there now. They've been emptied out by the police. What did they find? Nothing. No threatening notes, no love notes, no secret numbers to a game. Nothing. The guy knew what he was doing. Nothing telltale left behind."

"You worked together for a long time?" asked Mattheus.

"At least ten years," said Jeffries, his voice catching. "Come into my office. We'll talk."

"Let's talk in here," said Cindy. She enjoyed being in Paul's place, letting the vibration sink in, scanning his bookshelves, looking at the photos of Kendra and Nell. A sense of his life came over her here. The office showed a powerful man, successful, intelligent, attached to family. There wasn't yet a kink in the armor that she could see for herself.

Jeffries turned to Peggy then. "You can go back to the front desk now," he said.

Peggy nodded, turned and left.

"Okay," he said to Cindy, "let's sit down here and talk."

The three of them sat down as Jeffries started tapping his hands together.

"Miss the guy like hell," he said. "I still can't get it through my brain that he's gone for good. This never should have happened. I warned him lots of times to be careful, though. He loved the underworld too much. Got much too chummy."

Cindy was taken aback. "How so?" she interjected.

Jeffries turned and looked at her; then he looked at Mattheus.

"We're a team," Mattheus said.

"Yeah," said Jeffries, "heard that Kendra wanted a woman detective on the job. She's always had a distrust of men. Except for Paul, of course."

"They had a good marriage?" asked Mattheus.

"As good as any," said Jeffries. "I know the cops are focusing on her, but that seems unlikely to me. I never saw bad blood between them. And he never complained about her to me. If Paul was one thing, he was loyal."

"Who do you think did it?" asked Mattheus plainly.

"If you ask me, it's one of the cons," said Jeffries. "They're a tricky bunch. You're playing with fire when you take on these cases." Jeffries scraped his throat loudly.

"You ever had any trouble with them personally?" asked Mattheus

"No, I haven't, but I always thought the day would come. Not to Paul, but to me. I'm shorter with them. I can get nasty."

"You want me to go through your cases as well as his?" asked Mattheus.

"It's not necessary," said Jeffries. "We kept our cases apart. Stick with his."

"What else can you tell us about him?" asked Cindy. She felt that this guy knew a lot more than he was letting on.

Jeffries got antsy. "What do you want to know? Paul lived big and gave a lot. Big tipper, too. You'd always see him in his expensive suits, driving his yellow car. The guy didn't like to stay in one place for too long or be pinned down. He loved to come and go. Did a lot of work in St. Croix, so he'd fly out for a couple of days and then fly back home. It was a way of life for him. Everyone got used to it."

"Peggy said he loved his work, and his clients?"

"Sure," said Jeffries. "The guys he helped loved him too. You can't do this job if you don't have some connection with them. Paul also liked being a big man around town, having influence in the courts and with the cops. His word had weight. He was respected. No one could believe that he'd been found dead like that. In a back alley, like a heap of trash! It didn't fit. I really would have thought the cops would have done a better job hunting for his killer."

"We're on the job now," said Cindy.

Jeffries looked at her, amused. "Okay," he said, "don't hesitate to call me if you need anything else." He chuckled. "Or if someone else suddenly turns up dead."

CHAPTER 12

Mattheus went back to the police station to do more research on Paul's past clients and Cindy felt it was time to drive to the address Heather gave her.

She went back to the hotel and called for her car. When it arrived, she got in and began to drive slowly to the address Heather had scrawled on that piece of paper. Bright sun pierced the windshield and she turned the radio on loud to lift her spirits as she drove. Lively reggae music came on and Cindy sang along with it. It was easy to feel good down here. For a brief second she wished Mattheus was with her, sharing the drive and music.

The address she was headed to was all the way on the eastern tip of the island. It was almost a world apart, a residential community that dipped down along the ocean. Some said it was an island of its own. Cindy was more comfortable driving now as she learned how to navigate the treacherous, winding roads. This work was exciting. Every day she learned something new and met someone else that expanded her mind. Now she enjoyed the changing scenery, as the ocean came into view and then disappeared again behind a clump of trees. As she wound her way to this distant peninsula, she looked forward to what and who she would meet next.

Heather had told her the person would tell her all she needed to know. Cindy didn't take that so seriously. At times it was hard to take anything too seriously here, with the warm breezes, beautiful ocean, and endless flowers that greeted you wherever you went. The case seemed elusive and confusing still, with nothing that she could bite into. But Kendra's life could be in danger if Cindy didn't find something significant soon. Cindy didn't sense that Kendra was a killer, but she'd been wrong before and was holding all options open now.

As the car approached the destination, the roads and streets smoothed out. Cindy drove through small, winding lanes until she came to the back entrance of the community and was able to drive in. She then drove slowly along the manicured pathways. This was definitely a world set apart, one that seemed to enjoy keeping others out, being secluded, and making sure everything stayed the way it had always been. The beautiful, well-appointed homes were nestled between old trees, surrounded by beautiful lawns and gardens. They seemed as if nothing had touched them ever, or ever could.

After a few more blocks, finally, Cindy came to the address she'd been given. It was a pale beige stucco house, set off the street, behind huge palm trees. Cindy parked outside, got out, and looked around. For as far as the eye could see, there was nobody.

Cindy walked up to the front entrance. There was a huge, copper knocker on the front door, with a carved woman on it. For a second, Cindy pulled her hand back. Then she laughed, lifted her hand to the knocker, and knocked loudly. The sound rang out through the quiet block.

In a few moments, a beautiful, exquisitely groomed woman in her late forties, with huge green eyes, soft brown hair, and perfect skin, opened the door. She looked at Cindy curiously.

"Yes?" she said, standing at the door.

"I'm Cindy Blaine," said Cindy.

The woman made no response, just kept gazing.

"Heather May gave me your address," Cindy went on.

The woman's eyebrows rose slightly.

"I apologize for disturbing you, but may I take a few minutes of your time?" asked Cindy.

"What is this about?" asked the woman.

"I'm investigating a case on the island," Cindy said.

The woman seemed completely uninterested. "I don't know anything about cases on the island," she said. "We live quietly here and don't pay attention to the messes all around."

"I can see that."

Cindy smiled, but the woman didn't respond.

"I'm investigating a murder that took place a short while ago." Cindy spoke with greater urgency.

The woman shivered a moment. "Awful," she said.

"Yes, awful," said Cindy. "And I need to talk to you for just a few minutes."

"Why me?" The woman seemed truly disconcerted. "I have nothing to tell you about any murder."

"But you may know something that will lead me closer," said Cindy definitively. "Heather May said you might be able to."

The woman looked perturbed and shook her head. "I barely know Heather May."

"Just for a few minutes."

Reluctantly, she opened the door a little wider and let Cindy in.

The home was gorgeous, immaculate, perfectly decorated. The woman showed Cindy into the main sitting room and both of them sat opposite one another in high-back wooden chairs.

"I let you in because Heather May sent you," the woman said quietly. "Even though I barely know her, she's rather close to a dear friend of mine. My name is Margot Kowan."

"Pleased to meet you," said Cindy, looking around. "Your place is truly beautiful."

"Thank you," said Margot. "It's a great relief to be here, apart from the turbulence of the main island."

Cindy could see how she would feel that way. "You live here with your family?" Cindy asked.

"With my husband and son," said Margot, speaking matter-of-factly, with little emotion.

"Your husband works down here on the island?"

"What difference does that make?"

Talking to her was like talking to an ice glacier. Cindy needed some way to make contact and felt as if she couldn't get through. She decided to speak to her straight.

"Heather told me that when I came to this address, I'd know all I needed to know about the murder that took place on the mainland," Cindy said.

Margot's eyes opened wide. "I can't imagine why she'd say a thing like that. As I told you, we hardly bother down here with what happens on the mainland. This is our own little world. We like to keep it that way." She spoke quickly and breathlessly.

A long chill went up Cindy's spine. Margot lived in an encapsulated bubble and didn't want anything bursting it. She had no interest at all in being drawn into something that was painful or sordid. Cindy decided to try another tack.

"How do you know Heather May?" she asked.

"As I mentioned, she's a friend of a friend. The friend thinks the world of her. I've met Heather once or twice. Seemed like a wild card to me. The hair, I mean," and she smiled slowly. Everything about Margot and her home were in perfect order, not a thread out of place. Cindy could see why Heather would make her uneasy. Cindy felt she couldn't find an entranceway into any of Margot's true feelings at all.

Just then the large French doors leading to the sitting room opened, and a tall, lanky young man walked in. He had dark hair, dark eyebrows, and a sculpted face that reminded Cindy of someone, but she couldn't pinpoint exactly who.

"This is my son, Graham," Margot said quietly.

Graham looked over at Cindy and smiled shyly.

"Cindy has come to talk to us about matters from the island," Margot said to him. "Seems there was a murder there recently, and she's trying to find out more."

Graham flinched.

Cindy noticed with surprise how sensitive he was. "I'm sorry to come and disturb you," she said.

"Who was murdered?" asked Graham, ill at ease.

"A man named Paul Robbins," said Cindy. "A pretty well-known criminal defense lawyer. Have you heard of him?"

Graham shook his head and so did Margot.

There seemed little else to be said or done here. Cindy couldn't help wondering why in the world Heather had given her this address.

Graham turned his back to Cindy then and started walking away.

Cindy didn't want him to leave. He seemed more available than his mother. "Do you spend time on the main island, Graham?" Cindy asked.

"Graham goes to high school on the main island now," Margot answered for him. "All the children in this area commute there for high school. Graham is a senior now and has spent the past four years there."

"And after high school?" Cindy tried to make conversation with him.

"That is exactly what his father and I are trying to decide now," Margot said and stood up, as if to announce that the interview was over.

"Will his father be here later on this evening?" Cindy asked, suddenly curious to meet him.

"He's out of town for a few weeks right now on business," said Margot, irritated. "Why?"

Graham turned and looked back at Cindy then, over his shoulder. "He's away on business most of the time," Graham said, sullenly.

Margot didn't like that. "But he provides a wonderful life for you, Graham. For both of us."

Graham turned back then and continued walking to where he'd been headed, soon leaving the room.

Margot sighed. "He can be difficult at times," she said, "recalcitrant. Teenagers are that way often, I hear. He was perfect as a child growing up, though, never said or did a thing to upset us."

"Everything changes," remarked Cindy, "it can't be helped."

Margot seemed to like that. "You can say that again," she said with more intensity. "Listen, I'm sorry I can't be of more help. I just don't know anything about what you're doing. I have no idea why Heather sent you to me. My guess is that she can be a trickster at times. Gets pleasure out of creating dramas. It's something I sensed the first time I met her. I wouldn't take what she says too seriously. I have no idea what my friend sees in her at all."

Cindy had briefly thought the same thing herself. "Of course," said Cindy, "I understand."

That seemed to relieve Margot even more. "Come on, let me show you around," she said then. "I don't want your trip to be entirely worthless."

"It wasn't worthless," said Cindy. "It was nice meeting you and Graham."

Margot seemed touched by Cindy's comment and smiled warmly. "How lovely of you to say that. Let me show you around. Perhaps something will strike you."

Cindy got up and followed Margot through the majestic rooms.

"This painting is from the Gornigor collection," Margot started, bringing Cindy to a huge impressionistic oil painting that hung on the far wall. "This other one, across from it, is from the Rudon gallery."

Cindy looked at both of them. They had power, passion, majesty. Then something else caught her eye. Over on a thick, mahogany table, under the window, were some photographs framed in antique gold. Cindy went over to look at them more closely. As she got closer, she stopped and stared, unable to move from the spot.

"Who's that?" asked Cindy when she could finally speak.

"Just my husband, Gregg, myself, and Graham," said Margot. "Why?"

"This is your husband?" asked Cindy, dumbfounded.

"Yes, of course. What are you getting at?"

Cindy stared at the photograph over and over, and then looked at Margot, her heart pounding.

"When was that photograph taken?" asked Cindy, when she could finally get her voice to speak.

"What's wrong with you?" Margot asked, nervous. "It's a routine photo. I have lots of them. We took that one a couple of months ago."

"Does your husband have a twin brother?" asked Cindy.

"Of course not," said Margot irritated. "Tell me what is wrong!"

Cindy had no idea what to say. She stood there completely frozen. There was no question about it—the man in the photograph was Paul.

CHAPTER 13

"Do you mind if I step out a moment and make a call?" said Cindy, finally.

"Do whatever you want to," said Margot, who looked distressed now as well. "But tell me what's going on. Please."

Cindy didn't know what to say. "I will," she answered slowly, "but first let me make this call."

Cindy stepped out through the back door of the living room, into the blooming garden, and breathed deeply. She felt as though she were in a dream. How could this be possible? Was the man who Margot thought was her husband, just someone who looked like Paul? Cindy didn't think so. It was definitely him. She'd inspected his photo too many times.

Cindy took out her phone and quickly dialed Mattheus. Fortunately, he picked up instantly.

"Mattheus," Cindy gasped, having a hard time catching her breath.

"What's wrong?" Mattheus sounded alarmed.

"You've got to come here immediately."

"Why?"

"Paul had a second wife and family."

"What are you talking about?" Mattheus said.

"The woman I'm with is married to Paul. He has another name here, Gregg Kowan."

"Holy God," said Mattheus.

"And his wife has no idea he's missing. She thinks he's on vacation."

"She's nuts?" Mattheus asked.

"She's fragile," said Cindy. "Get over here. I don't want to tell her alone."

"Don't say anything," said Mattheus. "The police have to be notified. There are all kinds of steps we have to take. I'll contact them immediately, and then I'll get right there. In the meantime, don't leave the premises. Stay there and wait for me."

CHAPTER 14

Cindy hung up the phone and stood outside, not knowing how to proceed. She couldn't leave until Mattheus arrived, and she knew that Margot didn't want her to stay. She waited outside, lingering, trying to buy as much time as possible. It was actually beautiful and soothing to be out in the garden, which was filled with small cobblestone walks winding between beds of rich flowers. Over on the far side was a grape arbor with a small bench inside it. Cindy walked over to the arbor, went in, and sat down. Delightful breezes wafted through the enclosure, refreshing Cindy and soothing her mind. She wondered how long she could stay hidden here before Margot came looking for her.

To Cindy's surprise, as she sat, waiting, no one appeared. Cindy was left alone in the tranquil beauty of this home, which would soon be coming to an end. The man Margot thought she was married to was also married to someone else—and had a child with her as well! Cindy could barely absorb it. This turned the case on its heel. She had no idea how Margot would be able to handle the shocking news that lay in front of her. She seemed herself like one of the hothouse flowers, so carefully planted here. Although she'd seemed cold and distant in the beginning, as Margot relaxed and opened, Cindy developed a liking for her. She appeared to be a fine, delicate woman, who had just lived her life in a world of her own.

Margot's home would be about half an hour's drive for Mattheus. Cindy wondered how long she could really stay before Margot came to the arbor to find her. To Cindy's surprise, time passed uneventfully for what seemed like a long while. Then Cindy saw a shadow approaching on the ground, coming toward her. She stood up and walked to the edge of the arbor, as Graham approached. He stopped when he saw Cindy standing there in the shade.

"We wondered what became of you," said Graham, edgy.

Cindy looked at him closely now. Now she knew who he'd reminded her of! His father, Paul. It was shocking to realize that Paul not only had a second wife, but a son he'd been raising. There was also an intensity about Graham that Cindy found him interesting.

"I was just taking a moment's rest in the shade," she said. "I hope it's okay."

"It's fine," Graham answered, surprised. "My mother was looking for you, down at the other end of the garden. She said that you disappeared into thin air."

For no reason a pang of deep sorrow for Graham came over Cindy. As he looked at her, he suddenly seemed excruciatingly forlorn.

"I'm so sorry," said Cindy.

"About what?" Graham asked, his dark eyebrows curling. "And why did you really come to see us?"

Cindy saw that he couldn't really make out why she wanted to talk to his mother. It bothered him.

"Sometimes events have a life of their own," Cindy started to say, desperately wanting to prepare him also for what lay ahead. "Things happen that we can barely imagine. Our lives get turned upside down."

He listened more closely, his eyes slowly glistening. Cindy could see that he understood every word she said. She wondered if he'd had some sense of trouble.

"The more we struggle to get out of a bad situation," Cindy continued, "the more we can get trapped in it." She didn't know exactly why she was saying that to him, but he absorbed every word she said.

Just as he was about to respond, there was a crunch of noise behind him.

Margot arrived. "Well, here you are," she said to Cindy. "My goodness. I've been looking all over for you."

Cindy's heart began beating strongly. "I'm so sorry," she said, "it's so beautiful here. I couldn't resist stopping in and sitting down for a moment."

Margot looked at her strangely. "I find that odd, very odd."

"I'm terribly sorry," said Cindy.

"How long do you plan to stay?" Margot continued. "And what are you saying to my son?"

Margot was right not to go along, thought Cindy. She wasn't being straightforward. There was no reason to play these games with her, either.

"Listen," said Cindy, "when I called my partner, he asked me to stay here until he arrived."

Margot looked outraged. "I beg your pardon?" she said. Then she turned to Graham. "Graham, go to your room. There's absolutely no reason why you should be involved in this."

"I want to be here," he started.

"No, it isn't okay. Go to your room." Her voice took on a shrill, demanding edge that could not be easily turned down.

"Don't push me away," he said, nervous.

"I'm not pushing you anywhere, I'm just telling you to go."

Graham turned and walked away, throwing Cindy a long look over his shoulder.

"You have a wonderful son," said Cindy.

"It's irrelevant," said Margot. "You're not here on a personal visit. Who's your partner and what's going on?"

"My partner and I are private detectives," said Cindy.

Margot's hands tied into tight little fists. "And what has that got to do with me?"

Mattheus had told Cindy not to say anything until he arrived. He should be here any moment, Cindy figured. She'd pave the way for Margot slowly, start to prepare her for what lay ahead.

"You know there was a murder on the main island. My partner and I were called down to investigate it," Cindy began.

Margot's irritation seemed to grow. "So?" she said.

"Heather May told me I'd find out all I needed to know about the case right here."

"You're repeating yourself." Margot rubbed her foot on the ground, almost as if she were stamping out a bug that was annoying her. "We already said that was ridiculous."

"I didn't believe Heather either in the beginning," said Cindy. "But now I realize it was true."

Just at that moment, Graham came running back to the arbor, his face white. "Police cars are pulling up to the house, Mom," he called loudly.

"What?" Margot gasped.

"Come and see for yourself."

Margot turned and fled with Graham to the front of the house. Mattheus had arrived—he'd probably brought backup with him. This was a huge break in the case. It couldn't be kept under wraps long.

Cindy walked slowly back to the living room, dreading what was to come. By the time she arrived, Mattheus and three cops were surrounding the photos of Paul. Brayton was there, along with Nojo and another cop Cindy didn't recognize, who was taking pictures of everything. Margot stood near the sofa, terrified. Graham was nowhere to be seen—she'd probably sent him to his room again.

"Please sit down, miss," Brayton said to Margot.

"Not miss," said Margot icily. "Mrs. Gregory Kowan."

Mattheus came over and stood beside Cindy. "Great work," he whispered in her ear.

It felt good to hear that and to have him here.

Brayton held the photo of Paul in his hands.

"This intrusion is unacceptable," said Margot. "I'm going to call my husband right now." Her body began to tremble.

Brayton took pity on her for a second. "It won't be necessary," he said in a softer tone. "Just sit down a minute. We need to talk to you."

Margot obeyed automatically and sat on the edge of the sofa, upright.

"Listen, we don't mean to frighten you," Brayton went on. "But the guy in this picture is someone we're familiar with."

"You're familiar with my husband?" Margot's eyes flitted back and forth between everybody, unable to comprehend.

"You haven't seen the papers recently?" Brayton went on.

"What papers?" Margot asked, breathless. "I read our local papers. What have your papers got to do with anything? Has something happened to Gregg?"

"We know your husband by a different name."

Brayton was doing a fine job, thought Cindy. Nojo stood behind him for support, his face impassive, taking it all in.

"What name do you know my husband by?" Margot's voice started to teeter.

Brayton kept going evenly. "We know him as Paul Robbins, a well-known criminal defense attorney."

Deep confusion spread over Margot's eyes. "Who?"

"Paul Robbins was murdered about two weeks ago."

Margot stood up swiftly. "But Gregg Kowan was not."

"They're one and the same," said Brayton.

"This is ridiculous," Margot yelped. "Obviously, you have my husband mixed up with someone who looks just like him. My husband's fully alive, doing business right now on another island."

Cindy turned at that moment and saw Graham outside, at the edge of the door, crunched up against it, listening in.

"When did you last speak to your husband?" Brayton asked.

"When he left for his trip," said Margot, "about three weeks ago."

"You haven't spoken since? He didn't call you?" Brayton looked surprised.

"We weren't necessarily accustomed to speaking when he was out of town," said Margot. "It wasn't his way."

Brayton took a long breath and swallowed. "What kind of work was your husband in?"

"He imported and exported antiques and art objects," she said matter-of-factly, as if the world as she'd known it still existed. "He had a large business in many places—franchises."

"Were you close to your husband?" Brayton asked suddenly.

"I beg your pardon?" Margot bristled. "That's absolutely no business of yours."

"Just wondering how a husband can leave town for such a long time and not check in even one time?"

Cindy saw Mattheus look away.

"We did fine," said Margot. "We had our patterns and were happy with them." Then she stood up abruptly. "This is enough. You have to leave now. I'm exhausted. I want to call Gregg."

"I'm so sorry," said Brayton, "but we've got a long way to go."

"The man who was killed is not my husband," Margot said staunchly. "There's been a stupid mix-up of some kind."

"I wish that were true," said Brayton.

"It's this woman's fault." Margot turned shrill and furious to Cindy then. "You did this. You created this nightmare. Who asked you to come here and visit? I should have never let you in."

Cindy shriveled inside.

"My husband's alive," Margot demanded violently. "I'm calling him this instant and putting him on the phone. Then all of you will get out of here and never return."

She tore over to her phone, which was sitting on a carved end table, and dialed frantically. Obviously, a message machine picked up.

"Gregg, call me immediately. There's been an insane misunderstanding and I need you to call to straighten it up." Then she hung up. "He's not there now."

Cindy walked over to her. "Is there someone else you can call?" she asked kindly.

"I don't usually call anyone. I don't intrude in his life this way. How does it look to have your wife chasing him down?"

"It's an unusual circumstance," said Cindy gently.

"I can call his personal assistant." Margot was trembling.

"Good," said Cindy, "why not give a call?" She realized that it would be better for Margot to talk to others, slowly absorb the fact that her husband was no longer around.

Margot grabbed her phone again and started dialing. "You see what a humiliating position you're all putting me in."

Mattheus shook his head as Margot dialed, a look of pain crossing his face. The world he lived in and hers intermingled for a moment and he felt the torment Margot was going through. Cindy was touched to see him caring.

Margot clung to the phone as it rang and rang. Finally, someone picked up. “Wendy,” Margot said, breathless, “this is Margot Kowan.” She paused a moment and then went on quickly. “I have to get in touch with Gregg right away. We have a mini emergency here. No, it’s fine, no one is hurt. Do you happen to know where he is now?”

A long silence followed.

“Are you sure?” Margot continued weakly. “Really? What day exactly did he fly back? Well, no, he didn’t return home. No, I haven’t seen him. Please, wait a minute, don’t get frightened. I’m sure we can figure out where he is now. I’ll call you back later.”

Margot walked gingerly to the end table and put the phone down, just before her body slowly buckled, landing her on a nearby chair.

CHAPTER 15

"She said he left two and a half weeks, ago," Margot said in a tiny voice they barely could hear. "He told her he was going home."

"Do you live here alone?" Brayton asked softly.

"I live with my son." Margot sounded numb. "And the household staff."

"This is your son with your husband?"

"Of course," said Margot icily.

"She in any danger?" Nojo asked Brayton gruffly.

"Who knows?" Brayton replied. "Anything's possible now."

"I'll stay here with her a few days," Nojo offered.

Margot looked up at him, horrified. "No, thank you," she said. "It's not necessary." Then she looked over at Mattheus, who hadn't taken his eyes off her, but was absorbing her every single move.

"What do I need?" Margot asked Mattheus then. "A lawyer, detective? What happens now?"

Cindy moved in then and took over. "You can't stay here alone, with such shocking news. Do you have friends or family who can stay with you?"

"I have many friends," said Margot. "They'll come to my side. Are you telling me you think my husband has been killed?"

"That's part of it," said Cindy.

Mattheus came up close to both of them then. "You'll get the whole picture, little by little," he said. "There's a lot of questions you still have to answer."

Margot looked at him pleadingly. "I don't want to," she said.

"Maybe not this minute," Mattheus said, and turned to Brayton. "There's only so much a person can take. Give her some time."

"I can give her until tomorrow," said Brayton, "but we can't sit on this for long. We'll come back tomorrow, but first there's one thing we got to know."

"What is it?" asked Margot.

"What were you doing two weeks ago, the first Sunday of the month?"

Margot shivered. "The first Sunday of the month is when the book club meets at my home. Everyone was here with me all day..."

Brayton nodded. “Give Mattheus the name of some of the people who attended,” he said, “and we’ll call it a day. Tomorrow’s time enough to go forward.”

“Is there’s something else?” said Margot then, once again, trembling. “If there is, tell me now.”

“We may as well tell her,” Cindy said. “Better to hear it now when we’re all around. She’ll find out anyway, once this thing breaks open.”

“What is it?” Margot asked, her face contorting.

“Your husband had another wife and family,” Cindy slowly said. “He was known as Paul Kowan. They lived on the mainland.”

Margot just stared. “Another wife?” she mouthed silently.

“Double life,” said Mattheus softly.

Cindy turned once again then, and saw Graham clutching onto the edge of the open door. He’d been listening to every word. It was his father who had been killed as well.

“Come in,” Cindy called to Graham.

“Who’s that?” asked Brayton, suddenly seeing him.

“It’s the son,” said Cindy.

Graham walked in, went over to his mother, and stood behind her very close.

“We’ll get through this,” he said, in a hoarse ragged tone.

“And maybe we won’t,” said Margot.

CHAPTER 16

Mattheus drove home with Cindy in her car, the police car trailing behind them.

"You did it again," he said, grinning, "blew the case wide open."

Cindy was still in shock herself, and worried about Margot. "I don't like leaving Margot alone that way."

"She's got her son, and her friends are coming over."

Cindy said nothing. That might not be enough. Who knew how this news could affect her? In many ways she seemed so fragile. And then her striking bitterness came through. How could she not have been bitter, with her husband married to someone else all these years? And how could she not have known?

"I'm trying to figure out how a woman could not know that her husband had another wife and family, for years and years," Cindy said to Mattheus. "It defies the imagination."

"Most people fall into routines and think everything's great," said Mattheus. "Then it hits."

"But she had to feel it in some part of her being," Cindy insisted. "You didn't see how bitter she could get. And it's not only another wife, there are children in both families."

"I thought the woman was completely in shock," said Mattheus. "The police will go over her pretty good the next few days. They'll want everything she can tell them about Paul. Now we don't only have a defense attorney, we got a full-blown con man on our hands—and a whole other world he lived in. He fooled two women for years at the same time. Who else was he fooling?"

Cindy took a deep, painful breath. "He also had a fling with Heather," she said.

Mattheus grinned. "That's right. Jesus, this was one busy guy."

"Heather told me he meant a lot to her and that she ended their relationship suddenly."

Mattheus' ears perked up.

"Heather had to know about Kendra when she took up with Paul," Cindy went on, "so that wasn't the reason her relationship ended. When I asked her why, she told me to come here, and I'd find out everything I needed to know. Heather probably found out about Margot herself! It had to be too much for her. She had to realize the guy was a con. I'm going to spend more time talking to her."

"Talk to anyone you want," said Mattheus, "but Heather's just a sideliner. Kendra's the one who will suffer from this. This only adds new fuel to the fire. People are going to think that Kendra knew. She's smart, she's aware, runs her life like a pro. It would be harder to figure that Paul could fool her. There's more motive now. Maybe she found out and blackmailed him with that insurance policy? Or, she might have made him pay by buying her expensive jewelry? The other wife's just a pathetic character, sitting in a fancy home, in shock. He pulled the wool over her eyes completely."

"It's awful, awful," Cindy breathed. She felt as though she had just witnessed a life being wrecked before her eyes.

"No one said this was going to be easy," Mattheus said and put his hand over Cindy's for a moment.

It felt good to have his hand there. Cindy wanted him to keep it there.

"The work's rough, but you see what's real."

Cindy felt for the moment that she might rather not see what was real, stay sleeping, dreaming that the world was beautiful. Then she realized that was exactly how Margot had lived.

"I'm glad you came so over so quickly." Cindy suddenly turned to Mattheus, grateful.

"I'm glad you called," he said, touched.

Mattheus took his eyes off the road a second and looked at her warmly. They smiled at each other then, and it felt for a moment the way it had in Grenada, easy, warm, and secure. Cindy remembered then why she'd decided to work with him. She remembered how good it could feel.

"My guess is that the cops will be taking Kendra in pretty soon," Mattheus said. "More questioning is on the way. Could be they're close to locking her up."

Cindy's stomach clenched. "It's all circumstantial," she said.

"Yeah, but there's too much of it now," said Mattheus. "Comes to a point when enough is enough. It's probably a good idea for you to tell her in person about the second wife and family. Get her ready. See how she reacts. Sniff around the edges. Is it really possible that she had no idea?"

*

Cindy called Kendra and made arrangements to see her immediately, before she could hear the news from anyone else. This could be a terrible shock for her as well, thought Cindy. There was no reason to believe that Kendra had any idea about the second wife. Who knew how she would handle it?

Cindy parked in front of Kendra's home and came up the front walk, her palms growing sweaty as she got closer. Kendra opened the door, looking upbeat in an off-white linen dress with a sparkling, coral necklace around her neck, as if it were a normal afternoon.

"Come in," said Kendra, glad to see Cindy. "Let's go sit in the study."

The study was a large, square room filled with books, plants, and comfortable sofas. It felt snug and secluded from the sprawling outdoors. Kendra sat down opposite Cindy with a look of expectancy. It suddenly struck Cindy that she looked too perky and confident for the situation she was in. It was odd for a woman who was the focus of so much suspicion.

"It's been a while since we've spoken," Kendra started. "I know you've been very busy."

"Can't wait to hear what you've dug up. Someone out there did it, and they had to leave tracks around."

It seemed as if Kendra had no doubt at all that Cindy would find the information she needed to get her off. Perhaps the power of her conviction came from being totally innocent, Cindy wondered for a moment. Cindy decided not to jump in and tell Kendra the whole story, but see how much Kendra knew first.

"I met a fascinating woman," Cindy started. "Her name is Heather May."

Kendra showed no reaction at all.

"You know her?" Cindy asked.

Kendra shrugged lightly. "No, not really. I've heard her name, of course. We all vaguely know each other down here on the island, see each other in passing. But I've never spent any time with her. We've never actually talked."

That didn't completely make sense to Cindy.

"What about her?" Kendra was curious.

"She's quite a character," said Cindy.

"So what?" said Kendra. "There are lots of characters down here. That's why they chose this kind of life." She spoke as if she were at work, giving a guided tour of the island.

"Was Paul also a character?" asked Cindy.

"What difference does that make now?" asked Kendra, suddenly irritated. "He's dead. Someone killed him. And it wasn't me! I've been grilled enough. Now, I want you to tell me what you've found out."

"I will," said Cindy, "but I need to know more from you as well. It will help me put the puzzle together."

Kendra stood up and walked to the bookshelf. "Okay, what else do you want to know?"

"Whatever you can tell me about your marriage."

"What about you? Have you ever been married?" Kendra turned the tables on Cindy. "Do you know what it's like to live with one man, year after year after year?"

Cindy flushed, taken aback. "I've been married," she answered quietly. "But it didn't last long."

Kendra threw Cindy a sharp look with a mixture of pity and disdain. "So you get it," she said, "marriages fall apart. But unlike others, no matter what happened, Paul and I stuck it out. That's something I'm proud of."

"What did happen? "asked Cindy quick on the uptake.

"I told you before. He spent time at that bar, traveled for business, liked to gamble, I wondered if there wasn't another woman filling in the gaps. Can you understand that?"

"Of course I can," said Cindy.

"Is that what happened to you and your husband too?" Kendra arched her neck back, a dash of spite pouring from her eyes.

"My husband was killed," Cindy said calmly.

Kendra took a swift breath.

"On our honeymoon," said Cindy, trying to create a bond between them and getting Kendra to trust her more.

"My God, I'm so sorry," said Kendra, backing down. "I didn't mean to say anything nasty, I'm just so sick of being grilled and grilled."

"It's all right," said Cindy.

"Do you do this work because your husband was killed?" Kendra asked.

"Partially," said Cindy. "And partially I have a nose for it. It feels good to bring killers to justice. It's something important."

"I felt that immediately about you when I read about the case in Grenada," said Kendra.

"Kendra," Cindy said then straightforwardly, "you must have known that Paul played around."

"I wasn't sure, I thought maybe?" said Kendra, smiling feebly.

"There were people who might have known," Cindy said. "Why didn't you ask them? Why did you wait for me all these years?"

"How could I shame myself that way?" Kendra said.

"Heather May suggested that I see a woman down at the edge of the island who could fill me in on important details."

"Yes?" Kendra seemed interested.

"I went to the address she gave me and found a woman named Margot living there."

Kendra showed absolutely no reaction.

"You don't happen to know her?"

"No, I don't know anyone named Margot."

"Margot Kowan?" said Cindy.

"Who is she?"

There was no other way to tell her, than directly. "Paul had another wife and family all the time he was married to you. This woman Margot has his pictures all over, with her and their son."

Kendra looked as if she'd been doused with ice water. She shivered and then burst out, alarmed, "What kind of crap are you telling me?"

"Paul lived under an alias, Gregg Kowan."

Kendra stood up, her face turning beet red and her eyes flaming.

"This is crazy," she said. "You're a maniac! I should fire you for saying something like this." Her voice rose like a wild, shrill bird that had flown in the window and had no place to land. "And if you keep up like this, I will fire you. Now, get out!"

She kept yelling, until the door to the library flew open and Nell stood there, staring in. Once the door opened, Kendra took the opportunity to rush out.

"What happened?" Nell asked in an even tone.

"I had painful information for your mother."

Nell stared at Cindy. "What?"

"Something a woman named Heather May told me," said Cindy.

"Heather speaks to my mother all the time. What could she have told you that was different?"

Cindy stepped back. "What did you say?"

Nell looked confused. "Nothing, I just said that Heather May and my mother speak all the time. I can't see what could have so upset her?"

A long, slow chill ran through Cindy's arms. Kendra had lied to her about Heather May. What else was she lying about?

"Your mother and Heather are good friends?" Cindy asked.

"I wouldn't say that. They have lunch together occasionally and talk on the phone. Everyone knows everyone down here. There really aren't so many secrets."

Cindy liked Nell very much. She had a plain, forthright quality that Cindy appreciated.

"When your mother calms down, tell her to call me," said Cindy, definitively. She didn't like being played for a fool. There was no point to it.

Nell smiled oddly. "It won't make a difference what I tell my mother. She won't listen to anything I say. She never would. Don't let her stupid moods scare you. Be strong! Call her yourself!"

CHAPTER 17

All the way back to the hotel in the car, Cindy thought about the lie Kendra had told her. What could it possibly imply? Why did she say she hadn't spoken to Heather? What was she really covering up?

Cindy pulled over to the side of the road, took out her cell phone, and put in a call to Heather. She had to know right away whether Kendra knew about Margot. Everything could turn on this.

To Cindy's great delight, Heather picked up the phone immediately.

"Heather, this is Cindy," she said.

"Yeah, hi," said Heather.

"Thank you for sending me to that address. It was incredible."

Heather seemed disinterested. "Happy I could be of help. Got to go now."

Cindy clutched onto the phone. "No, wait a minute, please. Just one second."

Heather was in a hurry. "What?" She seemed put upon.

Cindy got straight to the point. "Does Kendra know about Margot?"

Heather was jarred. "Why would you ask me something like that?"

Cindy was stunned. Heather had been so helpful and forthcoming. Something had intervened. Someone had gotten to her?

"I thought you would know, since you knew about Margot."

"What has one thing got to do with another?" Heather said. "These are two separate women with two separate lives. Why would I get in the middle of them? Their lives have nothing to do with me." She sounded irritated.

Cindy was truly startled. "Has someone told you not to talk to me?" she said.

This only increased Heather's agitation. "Like who?" she snapped. "I don't know who you're talking to, or what you're thinking, but I'm asking you to leave me out of this now! I don't want you to call me anymore. I gave you a lead. That's it. I'm done now." And she hung up the phone.

Cindy sat staring at the phone in her hand. This was another game changer. Someone had clearly told Heather to back out and shut up. She'd been completely different when Cindy met her in person.

*

When Cindy returned to the hotel Mattheus was waiting for her in the dining room, sitting at a table in the front. Cindy sat down without a moment's hesitation and Mattheus looked pleased to see her.

"Whew," he said, "you look shot from cannon. Did you tell Kendra the news?"

"Yes, I did," said Cindy.

"She reacted badly to it?" He was tapping his fingers on the table, taking every word in.

"That's putting it mildly," said Cindy. "She screamed and yelled about it, but something worse happened."

"What?" Mattheus sat up straight.

"Kendra lied to me."

He let out a long slow breath. "About what?" he said.

"She told me she never spoke to Heather. Then, after Kendra left, Nell came in and told me her mother and Heather spoke frequently."

"Upsetting," said Mattheus.

"That's only half of it." Cindy was speaking quickly, heatedly. She hadn't processed any of it yet, and had enough to handle without having her head twisted around by Kendra. "I then called Heather right after I left to find out if Kendra and Margot knew about each other. Heather was a completely different person. Wouldn't say a word, just brushed me off."

"Par for the course," said Mattheus. "People fluctuate. Sometimes you catch them at an open moment, or you have to get them to that place. Then they get scared and close up again."

"Scared of what?" asked Cindy.

"Heather's probably afraid of being implicated. No one wants to get too involved. Especially when it's murder."

"This tells me that there's more going on between Kendra and Heather than I thought."

"Probably," said Mattheus.

"Do you think Heather told Kendra about Margot?"

"Good chance," said Mattheus, "but that won't do us any good. We need solid evidence. Gossip between women has a way of turning into smoke. It's Kendra's lie that I don't like."

Cindy suddenly felt exhausted. She pushed her hair back off her face, which was moist with perspiration.

"If Kendra knows about Margot it's a whole new ball game," Cindy said.

"Don't jump to conclusions," Mattheus said. "There can be lots of reasons why she might know and never say a word. Or why she might lie to you."

Cindy liked that. She liked the way Mattheus stepped back and let the process have sway. He didn't jump to conclusions like she did. Cindy admired the way he'd give up a theory on the spot as soon as he got evidence that was contrary.

"You're a scientist," Cindy said slowly.

Mattheus laughed. He seemed to like that. "You could say that," he said, "scientist of the mind and heart."

Cindy felt more at ease just sitting here with him, knowing she didn't have to deal with all that was happening alone.

"Let's go over it all again from the beginning," he said quietly. "If Kendra lied about Heather we're on a whole new path. You know, the police are pretty convinced it's her."

"I know," said Cindy, "but I'm not. When I finally told her about the second wife, she really freaked out. Told me to get out of the house. I don't think she had the slightest idea."

"No one seems to," said Mattheus. "I mentioned it to Roomey and his eyes bulged out of his head. This is shocking to everyone."

"Heather May knew, though," Cindy went on. "She sent me to Margot's house."

"Right," said Mattheus. "And the police are taking the tack that Paul's death is related to his having two wives. They feel that Kendra found out."

"They have no evidence."

"Not yet," said Mattheus.

Cindy and Mattheus looked at each other, as Mattheus shook his head. "It's amazing that you found out that Kendra lied, though. This is big. Look at that, you did it again."

"Beginner's luck," said Cindy.

"No," said Mattheus, "it's more than luck. You drew this to you. That's how all good detectives work. The information they need pulls them to it. There's a force out there looking after you."

Cindy loved the way Mattheus put things, she loved sitting here with him, the cool breezes from the ocean wafting across them as they spoke. But it was painful going through this situation. Even though things looked awful for Kendra, deep within Cindy didn't believe she'd killed Paul. There was something else floating around in Cindy's mind, though she couldn't yet say just what.

"I feel terrible adding to this suspicion about Kendra," Cindy said to Mattheus.

"We're here to find the truth," he said.

"But I don't think she did it," Cindy said. "She lied for another reason. Maybe, even though she suspected it, she was ashamed that Paul actually had an affair, and was covering it up."

Mattheus reached over and put his hand over hers briefly. "You're doing a wonderful job. You can't feel bad about what you find. I'm going to check in with the police and let them know what we've found."

Cindy felt agitated. "Don't tell them that she lied yet. Give it some time. After all, Kendra hired us."

"We can't conceal evidence," said Mattheus. "You have to trust that what is right will happen."

Cindy knew that he was right, but she couldn't trust anything with the police. They were dying to grab Kendra and string her up. Cindy felt herself sinking at the thought of it. Then she looked up into Mattheus' beautiful eyes. He had a way of lifting her spirits that she hadn't experienced for a long while.

Cindy tried one more time, though. "Listen, Mattheus," she said, "before you tell the police that Kendra lied to me, finish checking on Paul's clients. The answer to his murder could be there. It's not fair to keep piling on suspicion about Kendra until you've cleared that up."

Mattheus smiled at her broadly. "I love how loyal you are," he said. "I love that you don't give up."

Cindy's heart lifted again. "If you find just one guy who had a strong motive to kill him, that could turn things around. Otherwise we're only tightening the noose around Kendra's neck."

"We're not tightening the noose, she is!" said Mattheus. "At a time like this, what the hell right does she have to lie?"

CHAPTER 18

The minute Mattheus walked into the police station, a low cheer went up.

"Great work, Mattheus," Brayton called out. He was sitting at the desk with Nojo, going over stacks of papers. "Come on over, sit down. This is a damn treasure chest."

Mattheus went over and joined them.

"Who could ever have imagined the guy had a second family? You would think one would be enough for any man," Brayton said as Mattheus sat down.

Brayton and Nojo laughed.

"The other wife, Margot, is a good woman, too," Brayton continued. "She opened her home to us, let us go through all the papers we needed. Looks like she's a great mom to the son, too."

"Can't be sure about that," Mattheus interjected. These guys made up their minds much too fast.

Nojo shook his head. "No, this woman is different from the others. You can see it right away. Not about to twist you and turn you."

Brayton laughed again. "Looks like Nojo's got a shiner for this dame."

Nojo grunted uncomfortably.

"Well," said Mattheus, "glad you like her, but whatever you see at first, it's usually upside down. Here we thought this guy Paul was a regular chap and it turns out he's crazier than the rest."

"You can say that again," said Brayton. "Who the hell needs two wives when women around here are a dime a dozen?"

"Must have enjoyed the con," asked Mattheus.

"Big time," said Brayton. "Can't say the guy wasn't smart though. Did a great job with the hoods he defended. Got most of them off, too. I always thought he enjoyed it too much, though."

Nojo snorted. "Don't know how he got himself a wife like Margot, either. Boy, she's gonna help us nail the other one—and good."

That jogged Mattheus' memory. He'd made a promise to Cindy he wanted to keep.

“Don’t be so sure about Kendra,” said Mattheus. “I need more time to find out about Paul’s clients. I’m not done with my search.”

“Search all you want,” Brayton said. “From the looks of things now, Kendra’s the one. And what did your other search come up with? Roomey Burke, who everyone knows, and Silbert Hours, of all people!”

All the guys started laughing.

“The best-known pimp in these parts. And where was he when Paul was killed? In bed with his ladies, all afternoon. We got one after another to vouch for him.”

The guys laughed harder.

“All right, you guys.” Mattheus grinned, moving away. “I’m going to see what I can dig up now about Paul’s clients.”

“Won’t be much better than that,” Brayton said.

“Man, this is a huge waste of time,” Nojo grumbled.

“Time’s one thing I can’t waste.” Mattheus grinned again.

“You want to make the boys look bad?” Nojo looked at him under a crinkled forehead.

“Hey, it’s my job to look in the corners you guys don’t have time for,” Mattheus said. If something comes up, it’ll make you look good.”

Nojo laughed. “Want to make me look good? Find me a broad I can take home to mamma.”

Mattheus laughed out loud. It was hard to imagine that Nojo had a mother who would want to see his girlfriend. “One of these days it’ll happen, Nojo.”

“Yeah, when Paul comes back from the dead.”

Mattheus went to the computers in the back of the room, sat down at the desk, and opened one up. He had the password to Paul’s professional files and it wasn’t hard bringing everything up. Mattheus searched for a list of the clients who’d lost their cases in the past two years. Surprisingly, there were only a few of them. Paul had been a hell of a defense lawyer.

Mattheus took down the names, addresses, and histories of the clients who’d lost. They’d all been sent to jail. He then looked further at their sentences. Mattheus wondered again why in hell anyone would defend low-lifes like these. What did it say about guys who defended them? Mattheus could never come to terms with it. Once he said that to some cops in Grenada and it didn’t go over well.

“What in hell are you suggesting?” they’d said. “Everyone’s got a right to a defense. It’s the law.”

Mattheus didn't say anything, but deep down, he didn't agree. There was a natural law too, that got rid of poison, knew how to wipe it away. Mattheus could smell a killer a mile away, especially someone who could slit his girlfriend's throat. A bastard like that deserves to die.

Mattheus scanned the list of Paul's cases. Seemed he only lost about five percent of them. The rest got off scot-free. Clearly, Paul had good relationships with the cops and judges. Mattheus wondered about the cases he lost. What had happened? Most of guys were still sitting in jail. One wasn't! He popped out immediately—Salmon Abels, released on probation two weeks before Paul's murder. Mattheus let out a long, slow whistle. This was hot—something to explore. He dug in further, looking up a record of the trial. Abels had been accused of slitting his girlfriend's throat a couple of years ago and went to jail. Mattheus was shocked that he'd been let out on probation now. The case was entirely circumstantial; there was not one piece of evidence linking him to the crime. And the case didn't go to court. Paul had arranged a deal for a lesser sentence. There'd been lots of questions about what had happened.

Once the deal was made, the guy kept saying he'd been hoodwinked into it because he was scared. He was completely innocent. He blamed his rotten luck on Paul right from the start. Once in jail he created a little stir, yelling that he was innocent, gathering a few public supporters, demanding an appeal.

Mattheus read further. The case only seemed to have had nuisance value for Paul. He'd responded to the guy's pleas a few times, refusing to do the appeal. Paul told Abels he'd gotten a great deal and would be out with good behavior in a few years. Paul seemed to know something the guy didn't know, and that was something that didn't make sense to Mattheus either. He wondered about it. When Paul kept refusing to appeal, the guy finally found someone else, who got him out on probation. And Abels had been let out on probation two weeks before Paul was killed!

"Sweet Jesus," Mattheus breathed. "It isn't possible!" Mattheus let out a long, slow whistle. He couldn't believe his eyes. This could be the missing link. These guys got crazy in jail with nothing to do but dwell on the people they thought did them wrong.

"Hey, guys." Mattheus let out a holler. "Get over here this second!"

The shrill urgency in his voice pulled Brayton and others right to him.

"Salmon Abels," Mattheus uttered, "convicted killer client of Paul's, let out on probation two weeks before he died."

"Coincidence," said Brayton, "nothing to get excited about."

The guy talked in jail—blamed Paul for it," said Mattheus.

"They all got to blame someone," Nojo said. "That's why they end up in jail."

"I'm going to check out this dude, face to face," said Mattheus, eager to get to him.

Mattheus saw Nojo's eyes turn to slits as he looked at Mattheus. He probably feels my hate, thought Mattheus. Probably knows how badly I'd like to get my hands on this guy—teach him a lesson. Mattheus wasn't ashamed of any of it. Justice comes with different faces, he thought. Best when it happens naturally, like a tiger stalking its prey.

"This is a detour and waste of time," said Brayton. "There's plenty you can help us do to finish nailing Kendra."

Mattheus loved manhunts, circling a trapped criminal, weaving a web, drawing him in. He especially loved the moment they got him close, so he could look into the guy's eyes as he knew his time was up. The blood in Mattheus' veins began to boil. He thought of the hunts he'd been on for his wife's killer, and how they'd come to nothing. Mattheus had gone round and round again in circles trying to track the killer down. The guy was sure-footed and tricky though, knew each step of his way, disappeared into thin air. Some said he was hiding in plain sight. Mattheus didn't accept any of it. It took Mattheus a year to stop tracking him. The guy was still out there, though. Mattheus knew he'd never rest easy until he was found.

Brayton scraped his throat and looked at Mattheus long and hard. "Connecting this convict to our case is a long shot," he said. "If you ask me, it's a waste of time."

"Don't agree." Mattheus shook his head hard. "It's something you got to clear up before you nail Kendra. Otherwise there's reasonable doubt."

"What kind of doubt?" Brayton snarled, and started tapping the floor with his foot. "It's as clear as day. Kendra had to have found out about the other wife. How could she not have? She's one shrewd broad. And there's got to be evidence out there proving it. In fact, I'm sure there is." He looked long and hard at Mattheus.

"Maybe there is and maybe there isn't," said Mattheus, noncommittal. If he told them that Kendra had lied to Cindy, it would be all over in a second. Mattheus wasn't ready for the case to close, though, and neither was Cindy. There was more to dig up.

They both felt certain of it. And this escaped convict could be the missing link.

"I'm going to talk to Salmon Abels," Mattheus said.

"You're one stubborn dude," said Nojo.

"Better off staying here," said Brayton. "We could use anything else you could find on Kendra. We're setting up a meeting between her and Margot and having it recorded. They're going to lunch."

Mattheus wrinkled his nose. "I'm more interested in Salmon than listening in on two ladies at lunch."

Nojo laughed out loud, but Brayton wasn't having any part of that.

"We've already talked to Margot. She's willing to do it, even though it's not going to be easy for her."

Mattheus was surprised. Margot hadn't seemed like a woman who'd be willing to go out of her way.

"She's working with us—wants to find her husband's killer as bad as we do. She's agreed to wear a tape during her lunch with Kendra."

"Well, Cindy can step in and handle the ladies," said Mattheus. "Me—I want to look this killer straight in the eye."

"You and Cindy each know your place?" said Brayton, edgy.

"That's right," said Mattheus.

"Quite a team, aren't you?" said Brayton.

"The best on the islands," Mattheus grinned.

*

Mattheus' heart was beating as he went to the hotel to meet Cindy. He wanted to tell her about Salmon Abels in person. She was the one who'd pushed him to do it, and once again, she'd been right.

He got to the hotel and went out to the veranda, where she was waiting. It was cooler than usual, closer to the time the storms were coming. There were moments when Mattheus saw Cindy with fresh eyes. Right now she looked especially lovely, her hair blowing in the wind. He rushed over and sat down at her side.

"Get ready," he said.

Cindy's eyes opened wide.

"I found a client of Paul's who'd been sent to jail for murder who was let out on probation two weeks before Paul was killed."

Cindy gasped.

"Not only that he talked a lot in jail, said he blamed Paul for what happened."

"My God," breathed Cindy, "this could be it."

Mattheus watched her tremble as he spoke. It was touching to see how important it was to her to help Kendra.

"I've told the guys about it," said Mattheus, "and I'm going myself to check him out."

"Thank God," said Cindy again.

But Mattheus stopped her. "Not yet," he said, "don't get your hopes up. It's only a possibility." He knew from long experience, it was dangerous to pin your hopes on anything too soon. And it was easy to do. Too easy to focus in on someone you thought should be guilty and block everything else out.

"It's a strong possibility," said Cindy, "given his background."

"We don't know that," said Mattheus. "It sounds good on paper but you never know what you have until you meet them in person. He might have an airtight alibi for all we know."

Cindy took a deep breath. "He might. Because the police are going on full force with their investigation of Kendra. Brayton contacted her about having lunch with Margot," Cindy said. "Kendra said she'd only do it if I went along."

"Smart," said Mattheus, smiling. "She needs protection."

"At first Brayton balked," said Cindy, "but that was the only way Kendra would agree. In fact, the details of the lunch are being set up right now."

Mattheus thought about whether or not he should tell Cindy that Margot would be wearing a tape. He decided he had to. They were a team.

"Margot will be wearing a tape," said Mattheus then.

Cindy's eyes opened wide.

"Brayton is convinced Kendra knows stuff she's not saying. You can't tell Kendra about this though. The truth is the truth, let it all come out."

"Do you think I would undermine the investigation?" Cindy seemed offended.

"I wasn't saying that. I just wanted to say, let it all rip."

"I want to find the real killer as much as Brayton," Cindy said, unabashed. "I didn't come down here to assist a cover-up."

Mattheus was pleased that he and Cindy were on the same page about so many things. She was one special woman, for sure. And, of course, being a detective was different when someone close to you had been killed. After that, each case you handled was an echo of what happened. Your craving for justice couldn't be squelched.

"I'm proud of you, Cindy," Mattheus said then.
She was silent a moment. "For what?" she said.
"For who you are."
"Thank you," she said softly.
"I never expected all of this in one woman," he said.

CHAPTER 19

Cindy and Kendra walked to the lunch together. It was to be held at a lovely restaurant across from the main pier in town. A table had been reserved in the rear, overlooking a boat slip that was at the end of the dock.

Kendra, dressed a white linen suit, with her hair brushed back tight, had a formidable air about her. Her jaw was set and she said little. Cindy wore a simple lime green dress and pearl earrings.

"I've been thinking about why the police want Margot and I to meet so badly," Kendra said, finally. "Obviously, they're going to question her about everything I say. And question me about her. It's an old trick, isn't it, turning one against the other? They must be hoping that in the heat of the moment one of us will slip up."

"Or that one of you will lie," said Cindy. "That wouldn't look good, would it?"

Kendra said nothing then, just fell silent.

"Are you curious to meet her?" Cindy then asked to break the silence between them.

Kendra smirked. "Not really. "I'm only doing this in the hopes it will help clear me. Who knows? She may be involved with the murder herself. Nothing would surprise me."

Cindy took a deep breath. She felt uncomfortable accompanying Kendra to the lunch.

"I'm sure she's dying to meet me," Kendra went on bitterly. "But I have no self left to meet. They've taken it from me. This is the last straw. And the truth is, there's no reason I should validate whatever happened between those two and call it a marriage."

"It was a marriage," said Cindy. "She has the same marriage license you do."

"But to a different man, Gregg Kowan. It had to be a fraud."

"Paul operated with two identities," Cindy said, "and who knows how many more?"

"Whose side are you on?" Kendra snapped back.

"It's not a matter of sides," said Cindy. "Your husband has been killed. So has hers. It's the same person. The more we know about went on in his life the better chance we have of finding the killer. It's as simple as that."

"Nothing simple about it." Kendra was exasperated.

Cindy couldn't understand why she didn't feel more sympathy for Kendra, why few people did. Maybe because she seemed so unmoved about what happened to Paul. Cindy hadn't heard her express sorrow about his death once since she'd met her. But she'd been pounced on from day one; suspicions about her had never let up. She had every right to be brittle and mad.

"The police haven't grilled Margot the way they did me, "Kendra went on. "That pisses me off."

"How do you know they haven't?" said Cindy.

"It's obvious. They think I found out about the other wife, and took my revenge. But maybe she found out about me? Why isn't that equally possible? Why isn't she shaking in her boots?"

"Maybe she is," said Cindy.

"You haven't been grilling her either, have you?" Kendra turned to Cindy, swiftly. "Why not?"

Cindy paused a moment to consider that question. There was truth to what Kendra said. Cindy felt no desire to question Margot further. Margot had seemed so devastated when she'd found out about Paul that Cindy didn't doubt her. She didn't like her much, but she didn't doubt her either. It was interesting where suspicion landed and the reasons for it, Cindy thought.

"So give me a clue as to why I'm the bad one?" said Kendra, fitfully.

Cindy turned and faced her as they were about to enter the restaurant.

"Did you love your husband?" Cindy asked. "Or was it over a long time ago?"

"Go to hell," Kendra muttered. "You think I'm paying you for this?"

"Paul led a double life. You had to sense something. He couldn't have been there much for you. How could you not hate him?"

Kendra's face flushed, then turned ashen. "It's a complicated," she finally said. "Did I love him? Depends what you mean when you say love. And hate, that's a strong word. You have to care a lot to hate someone. Maybe all the embers between us had just died."

"Things don't just die," said Cindy. "People hurt each other a lot first."

"Are you crazy or something?" asked Kendra. "Pushing me up against the wall?"

"I'm pushing you because I want to clear you," said Cindy. "I want to get everything out on the table, turn it over in daylight, find out why it went on. The best way to be free is to be honest—especially with yourself."

Kendra turned to her. "You go be honest with yourself," she snarled between perfectly formed, small, white teeth. "Why the hell are you down here on the island, poking around, way out of your league? It was a mistake to ever hire you."

Cindy felt punched in the gut. At the same time it was fascinating to see how Kendra could turn on someone who was on her side, trying to help. Maybe she wanted to be found guilty? Maybe she actually committed the crime?

The restaurant was only half filled when they walked in, as it was still early. The moment Cindy and Kendra walked in, the maître d' was ready for them, and showed them to a table in a half-lit alcove in the rear, set away from others.

Kendra sat down and looked around anxiously. "Figures she wouldn't be here yet," she said. "It's extremely rude of her to make us wait. What kind of woman would make us do that?"

"We're a little early," said Cindy. She'd pulled herself back together, decided to be entirely professional, not take anything this woman said personally in any way.

Their water glasses were filled and they were given a wine list before the waiter left them alone.

"Why did you ask me if I loved Paul?" Kendra looked at Cindy oddly. "Are they thinking that Margot loved him and I did not?"

"I have no idea what they're thinking," said Cindy. "I do think she loved him, though."

Kendra shuddered. "Do you know how that feels? Hearing your husband was loved by another woman who thought she was his wife?"

"It has to be awful," said Cindy.

"Infuriating. I loved him in the beginning," said Kendra. "He changed over the years. So did I. We had a daughter, we had a home. I knew he wasn't perfect. But his having another wife and son is not something I ever imagined! It sticks in my craw. I'm not ready for this kind of public humiliation. The idiot ended up making me into a fool."

Cindy felt bad for her. "I'm very sorry," she said.

"So if I'm agitated about this, I have a right to be," Kendra continued.

"You certainly do," said Cindy.

At that very moment they looked over and saw a woman in a blue silk dress, graceful, perfectly coiffed, walking toward them haltingly. Around her neck, she wore a ruby necklace.

"There's the bitch," Kendra muttered under her breath. "And what the hell's she wearing?"

Both Cindy and Kendra stared at the necklace.

"That's mine," said Kendra. "It's the one I bought that the police couldn't find."

Cindy was completely startled. "Obviously Paul gave it to her," she said.

Kendra's mouth hung open. "The bastard took my necklace from the safe and gave it to his other wife. He deserves to be strung up!"

Margot came closer to the table.

Cindy stood up and extended her hand. "Hello, Margot."

Margot gave Cindy her hand.

"Kendra, this is Margot," Cindy introduced them.

The two women stared at each other for a moment as Margot sat down. Cindy wished she could get away. The tension was so thick it ran over her arms and legs. For a second she could hardly catch her breath.

"That's an incredible necklace you have there," said Kendra, staring at it with fire in her eyes. "Where did you get it?"

Margot lifted her hand and touched it lightly. "Gregg gave it to me for our anniversary," she said.

"It's my necklace," said Kendra.

"What are you talking about? I cherish it," said Margot, clutching it tightly.

Thankfully, at that moment the waiter came back with a wine list for Margot and they ordered a bottle of red wine.

"We have more important things to talk about," said Cindy, trying to deflect the tension and bring the lunch back on course. It was clear these two had never spoken.

"We have a common purpose being here," said Margot icily, "to find the person who killed Paul."

Kendra stiffened. "Why did he give you my necklace?" she murmured, staring at it. "It was mine. I bought it for myself."

"You bought yourself jewelry?" Margot looked shocked. "He didn't buy it for you? He bought me every piece I have."

"Who knows what else he stole it from?" said Kendra.

"Let's leave this for later, please," said Cindy. "This lunch could help find the killer."

"I've been the main suspect, right from the start. You know that, don't you?" Kendra turned to Margot disdainfully.

"That's what I've been told," said Margot.

"Been told? It's been in all the papers."

Margot pursed her lips. “We don’t really pay much attention to news on St. Thomas,” she said quietly.

Kendra grimaced. “You didn’t see any of the photos of Paul in the paper?” she asked bitingly. Clearly, she was off her game with Margot. The two of them were worlds apart and seeing the necklace on her had really thrown Kendra.

“No, I hadn’t seen any of the photos in the paper,” Margot answered, her eyes suddenly filling with tears.

Kendra stared at her deeply. “You had no idea your husband was married to me?”

“Did you have any idea he was married to me?” Margot countered, bristling.

For a flashing moment, the two of them looked straight in one another’s eyes.

“I thought he might be cheating.” Kendra held back no punches. “In fact, I thought it was likely. I always suspected he had a lover that he met regularly at the bar.”

Margot trembled at that thought. “Did he?” she asked faintly, aghast.

“Yes, he did,” Kendra said. “I’m convinced of it now. A woman named Heather.”

Margot gasped. “A mistress?”

“Someone who must have wanted him all to herself. No one could have him all to themselves though, could they?”

“I thought I did,” Margot said.

“You thought he was faithful to you?” Kendra was incredulous. She also seemed to enjoy seeing Margot squirm.

“Yes, I did think that,” Margot said, forcefully. “Why should I believe you?”

Kendra leaned her elbows on the table. “How could you really imagine that you were the only one, with all his nights away?”

“It was part of his work,” said Margot, “a lifelong pattern. He told me he loved me, over and over. I believed what he said. I had no reason not to. None at all.” She looked up at Kendra then, her mouth quivering. “Did you believe that he loved you?”

“This is twice today I’ve been asked that question,” said Kendra. “We’d been married for years. What has love got to do with it?”

Margot did not smile. “We were married for years as well. We have a son.”

Kendra stopped and took it in. “I know. I heard it, but it doesn’t compute.”

"A son he loved tremendously," said Margot. "A son who meant the world to him. He coached his games when he was around, took him snorkeling, brought him all kinds of gifts."

That silenced Kendra. "He had a daughter he loved very much too," she finally said slowly. "Seems he was quite the family man."

Margot did not smile at that. It seemed hard for her to even realize that Kendra and Paul had a child together. "This is completely grotesque," she said finally. "Those nights he was away, he was with you?"

"Some of them," Kendra replied. "Who knows who he was with at other times?"

"I was completely fooled," Margot said in a small voice then, "fooled for years."

"Conned," said Kendra.

"So were you." Margot looked at her sharply.

"You can say that if you want to," said Kendra, "but just because he was an idiot, I don't see myself as a victim. I lived a good life. I did what I liked."

The waiter brought the wine, poured it in their glasses, and all together they took a long drink. Cindy then took it upon herself to order for all of them, a large salad and mushrooms. No one else seemed to be in shape to look at the menu.

"What do you want to know about me?" Kendra asked Margot boldly then. "I know you came here to find out about me. So go ahead, ask away."

Margot could barely speak. "Nothing," she said under her breath. "I just want you to go away."

"Why? He's gone now," said Kendra. "We're not sharing him anymore."

"We never shared him," Margot burst out.

"Are you crazy?" asked Kendra. "Of course we did."

"He belonged to me alone!" said Margot, her voice suddenly rising an octave. "You had to just be something extra. He gave me the necklace, not you."

"I bought that necklace for myself. He stole it from my safe and gave it to you. It's stolen property you're wearing."

"Please, go away, I beg you," said Margot, trembling.

"I'm not going anywhere," said Kendra, in a dark tone, "particularly not to jail. Paul might have been a rotten liar, but I didn't kill him."

Margot stared at her. "I want to wake up and find this was a bad dream. I want my life back the way it was."

"So do I," said Kendra, "but that isn't happening. And it's not a dream, is it? Here we are, flesh and blood. Do you have any idea who killed him?"

Margot looked aghast. "I can't imagine why anyone would want to."

"Not even you?" Kendra prodded.

Margot looked at her disdainfully. "Of all the women he could have chosen, why in the world would he have chosen you? I'll never understand it. Never. I can understand why you'd have to buy your own jewelry, why he didn't get it for you. What could you have given him that I didn't?" She seemed totally bewildered and overwhelmed.

Suddenly, Kendra perked up.

"I know he married you first, but when I met him he was handsome, exciting, and told me he was single. And he couldn't leave me alone. We spent incredibly passionate nights together."

Margot put her hands over her ears. "Stop."

"I can't even imagine how he could have been married then. He was totally available."

"He wasn't available," Margot cried out. "He was married to me."

"But what kind of marriage did you have?" Kendra was pitiless, ripping away Margot's memories, one by one.

"Our marriage was quiet, loving, content," said Margot, gasping.

"It isn't possible," said Kendra. "Not the way he was with me, hungry like you can't believe."

"Shut up, you're disgusting," said Margot. "And we had a bond that was unbreakable. He always told me that. *You* were just something extra."

"Far from it!" Kendra leered. "He couldn't do without me. Not even for a day. Wherever he was he'd call me."

Margot stood up trembling. "I hate you," she hissed.

"Sit down, Margot," said Cindy, trying to calm both of them.

But Kendra wasn't finished. She leaned toward Margot ferociously. "Did you really love Paul? Was he good to you?"

Margot jumped back, startled. "I loved him very much. He was wonderful." Her voice rose an octave. "How about you? Did you really love him? Tell me the truth!"

"I loathed the bastard," Kendra uttered, "and I loathe him even more now."

Margot gasped and so did Cindy.

At just that moment, Cindy saw a young woman walking over toward the table, Kendra's daughter, Nell. Cindy was stunned to see her.

"This is our daughter," said Kendra as Nell grew closer. "She wanted to meet the woman who was married to her father all these years. What do you think this is doing to her?"

"You're blaming me for this?" Margot was horrified. "How do you think our son's feeling?"

Nell arrived at the table and came right up to Margot. "Exactly when did you marry my father?" she asked.

Margot put her hands over her eyes, but then took them down and swiftly stood up.

"Your father, your husband! It's all ridiculous! He belonged to me. He never said a word about either of you. And I never want to see or hear anything about either of you again!"

Then she spun around and fled at top speed, between the tables, out of the restaurant, like a spinning top that would never stop spinning.

"I'm sorry, Mom," Nell said. "That woman's completely nuts. She's vicious, on edge, half crazy. She's got to be the one who did it. It's obvious, isn't it?"

Kendra simply stood like a statue made of marble.

"Nothing at all is obvious," she finally said.

CHAPTER 20

Abels was working as a dishwasher in a small, greasy restaurant behind the mall. It was mid-afternoon when Mattheus got there and the heat of the day pressed down on him, making it hard to breathe. By now his shirt was soaked with perspiration, and the place was even hotter, food steaming on the grills.

"Looking for Salmon Abels," Mattheus said to the guy who greeted him.

"Who?" The guy looked confused.

A wall fan creaked as it barely managed to ground around.

"He just started working here," Mattheus continued. "Washing dishes."

"Oh," said the guy, "sure. One second—I'll bring him out."

Abels walked out, jittery. He was younger than Mattheus had imagined, scrawny with wild eyes. "What?" the guy asked, pissed off.

"Private investigator," Mattheus said.

"What you guys want from me now?" asked Abels.

"Just sit down with me in the back," said Mattheus, "it'll only take a few minutes."

Mattheus and Abels walked to two stools in the back of the place, facing each other. The slanty window high up on the wall was cranked half shut and it was hard to breathe. Sweat poured down Mattheus' face as he leaned in toward Salmon. Salmon's head hung down, his eyes glued to the floor.

"Pick up your head and look at me," Mattheus demanded. This could be it. He could have the killer right here, red-handed.

Abels raised his head just a little bit. Mattheus scrutinized his round face carefully. He was late thirties maybe, scrawny, bones shaking under his skin.

"Look up at me," Mattheus repeated.

Abels raised his eyes. There was a look of exhaustion. Mattheus could see he'd been through this many times.

"Even when you're free, you're not free," Abels muttered. "They come after you like a pack of thieves."

"You know what you're here for now, don't you?" Mattheus was going for the jugular.

"No." Abels bit his lip.

He was acting sassy, but he was scared, and their conversation was being recorded. If all went well, Mattheus could get a confession from him and the case would be closed.

"I'm out of the clinker," Abels said in a thin tone. "And you're trying to throw me back in."

"You got it all down pat," Mattheus said. "Pretty smart.

Abels smiled a crooked smile. "Could say I'm smart," he answered. "Most people think so. Then I got framed for a job I never did."

Mattheus wasn't getting taken in. "What did you get framed for?"

"Killing some lady." Salmon smirked.

"You do it?" Mattheus asked, chummy.

"No, "said Abels. "She was a fancy dame and they needed someone to pin it on fast. It was just before elections. So, they found me dealing drugs in the neighborhood. That was it. I had a record, so they jumped my bones and good."

Mattheus pushed his stool back slightly. "You had a pretty damn good lawyer though," he prodded, taking the conversation on a different track. "You think he'd go along with something like that?"

Abels leaned in close to him, like they were two conspirators exchanging notes. "That guy couldn't stand my guts."

Mattheus let out a long, slow whistle. "Then why the hell did he take on the case?"

"He had to. They told him to do it and it made him look good. That's all he cared about, looking good for the public. And keeping the cops happy and sweet. This guy got plenty of passes by looking good. He didn't give a hoot about me—let me fall right through the hole. I'm positive that he was in cahoots with the big boys on this one."

"Think so?" Mattheus said. This could go to his motive to take Paul down.

Abels stretched his neck upwards and rubbed his long hands over his bony face. "Yeah, I think so. I think they're all in cahoots. You too."

"Not me, mister." Mattheus took exception. If there was one thing he refused to do, it was to be in cahoots with anybody. "I work on my own."

It didn't seem to impress Abels, who scoffed.

"So you got out of jail and let your lawyer have it. Right?" Mattheus said. "Must have felt good to get back at him?"

Salmon looked confused. “What do you mean let him have it? I haven’t seen him since the trial.”

Mattheus edged closer, turned up the heat. The guy’s face was about two inches away.

“Don’t play dumb with me.” Mattheus smirked. He had this guy locked up in his mind, bound in chains, confessing the killing. Mattheus desperately wanted to hear him confess.

“How the hell could I see the lawyer?” Abels spit the words out.

“I mean you took him down, just like you did the lady.”

At that, Abels froze. His eyes shifted back and forth fast, as if he were trying to grab onto an apparition floating in front of his face.

“Wait a minute, now.” He was getting the gist of it.

“Wait for what?” Mattheus said. But Abels looked so confused that Mattheus suddenly wondered if this guy even knew that Paul had been found in a pool of blood, dead.

“Why should I wait another second?” Mattheus growled. “We waited long enough to get our hands on you. You got out of jail a couple of weeks before Paul was killed. Everyone knew you blamed him for what happened to you.”

“Holy Christ,” yelled Abels. “Someone killed Paul?” He started shaking bad then.

“Don’t act like you didn’t know it.” Mattheus stood right up against him.

“What the hell does that have to do with me?”

“You hated the dude. He lost your case.”

Abels laughed in Mattheus’ face as spittle ran down the side of his mouth. “I hate a lot of people, mister. It doesn’t mean I kill them.”

Mattheus stepped back, looking at the fear in his eyes. “Where were you on the first Sunday of the month?”

“Easy. The festival. That day I was with friends in St. Croix. A whole bunch of people were there. We celebrated and I went with them to a carnival that afternoon. Lots of people saw me there. I helped a guy in one of the booths. I’ll give you his name.”

Mattheus stepped back. The guy’s eyes were still darting around in his head.

“I’m a rotten lousy critter, man, I’m a thief, I’m a bastard, but I didn’t kill anyone. In fact, I feel awful that the dude died.”

“You feel awful?” Mattheus was mocking him.

“Listen.” Abels crept closer. “I noticed every day I saw him that something was bugging this guy bad. Very bad. One day I said to him, calm down, dude, what the hell's bothering you? Someone breathing down your back? He laughed in my face and said it was worse than that. I said, oh yeah, what? He said I'd never understand and I was lucky I never had any kids. Something in that guy's family was making him crazy. Big time. I don't know if that helps you?"

Mattheus took a few steps away, as a slow chill went up his spine. This guy had no way of knowing that Paul had two families, two sets of kids.

Mattheus' head spun around and around. He had to breathe, step back, take it easy. It was possible this guy didn't do it. Could be he'd tracked down another guy that amounted to nothing. Mattheus relented,

"You'll give me the names and addresses of all the people you were with on that day, also the booth you worked in at the carnival?"

"Definitely," said Salmon.

"In an hour or two we'll know if you're lying. If you're lying, man, it won't be good for you."

"I'm not lying," Salmon said.

Mattheus believed him, and his heart sank into his shoes.

*

By the time Mattheus called Cindy the alibi had already been checked. It was airtight, he told her. Salmon hadn't killed Paul. He hadn't been anywhere near the crime scene.

Cindy listened quietly. "This is a bummer," she said. "The police have already listened to Margot's tape recording of the lunch. They heard Kendra say she'd detested Paul. She's just been arrested. But before she went to jail, there was one last thing she did." Cindy paused, agitated.

"What?" said Mattheus.

"She fired both of us," said Cindy.

"That was stupid," said Mattheus. "She needs us more now."

"She doesn't think so," said Cindy.

"Meet me at the hotel," said Mattheus.

"In an hour," said Cindy, sounding entirely defeated.

CHAPTER 21

Cindy was thrilled to see Mattheus back at the hotel. He took her hand when she came into the lobby and gave her a little hug.

"Let's go get a drink before dinner," he suggested. "You look beautiful."

That was the last thing Cindy expected.

"Besides, we've got a lot to talk about." Mattheus collected himself quickly.

They went into the lounge, sat down, and ordered.

The drinks came and they each took theirs. Mattheus downed his quickly. Cindy looked up at him as he drank. He seemed a little nervous. Maybe because they'd been fired. Nobody likes that.

"She's not in her right mind," Cindy said, "that's why she fired us now."

"I don't care about that," said Mattheus. "People do all kinds of things in desperate moments. And besides, she didn't participate in her own defense. She lied to you."

"Did you tell the police that?" asked Cindy, horrified.

"No, I didn't," said Mattheus. "It must have been the tapes from the lunch that did it for them."

"I can't shake the feeling that Kendra didn't do it," Cindy continued.

"I don't disagree," said Mattheus, "but there's nowhere else to go. Salmon Abels was Kendra's best hope, and that went nowhere. There's nothing left."

"The case against her is all circumstantial," Cindy repeated. "They never found a weapon."

"A road is paved step by step," Mattheus said. "When all signs point in one direction…"

Cindy put her hand over his. "Kendra didn't do it," she said emphatically.

Mattheus became quiet. "That's a big statement. You've got to prove it."

"Kendra's nervous, outspoken, frazzled to the bone," said Cindy. "She may not always be likeable either, but I'm sure she didn't know anything about Margot. That's what they're all grabbing onto now. The motive was the second wife."

"Cindy." Mattheus stopped her. "The police spent more time talking to Heather. She told them that Kendra knew about Margot."

Cindy was dumbstruck. "She knew? I don't believe that. Heather has her own agenda. She's getting something out of this—had to be terrifically jealous of Kendra. Heather's framing her, left and right."

Mattheus raised his hand to call the waiter to get another drink.

Cindy drank her drink slowly. It had been getting cooler on the island the past few days and the rum and soda warmed her.

"So, if you don't think it's Kendra, what's your best guess?" Mattheus asked as he waited for his refill. "Heather?"

"I don't think so," said Cindy, "she's just getting a sick pleasure out of watching Kendra squirm. Maybe she thinks Kendra did it, hurt the man she loved. When Heather found out about second wife years ago, she let go of Paul completely. It hurt like hell, but she just dropped him."

"A strong lady," said Mattheus, "good judgment."

"It's not so easy to drop someone you love," Cindy said quietly.

"No, it isn't," said Mattheus. "I still go nuts at times thinking about Shelly."

"Your wife?" asked Cindy. This was the first time he'd mentioned her name.

"It was good, we were happy. I thought we would last forever. We would have, too. We both felt it right away, as soon as we met."

"I know how that is," said Cindy, remembering when she'd first met Clint. It was as if the world had opened up in front of her, bringing this incredible gift. It was only destined to be enjoyed for a short while, though.

"There's not one person in the world who can take Shelly's place, either," said Mattheus, looking away.

"Nobody has to take her place," Cindy said suddenly, a moment of clarity enveloping her. "Only, one day you might decide to make room in your heart for just one more."

Mattheus was stung. He looked at Cindy sadly for a long while.

"The part that's worst about it," he finally said, "is that I never found the guy who killed her. It drives me crazy. I can't forgive myself. He's out there, living his life, and this beautiful woman is completely gone."

"She's not gone. She's living inside you," Cindy spoke heatedly. She felt such warmth and empathy for Mattheus. Clint was living inside her, as well. She felt it strongly as she spoke, realizing Clint could never disappear. She'd carry him and his love with her wherever she went. It was a wonderful moment, realizing that.

Mattheus slid closer on the sofa. "You're an amazing woman, you know," he said softly.

Cindy, taken aback, trembled.

She took a deep breath. Each word he said restored her.

"We're lucky we have this work to do, and that we're doing it together."

Cindy wondered for a second if he would ever be able to get past that, put it down, for even a short while. And would that even be good for them?

Strong winds suddenly blew in on them, giving them a taste of what was to come. All day the papers had been warning that Hurricane Lola was coming their way. The paper said it was a category 1 warning, and to expect thunderous winds and rains. People were beginning to board up their homes already.

"We're going to have to get out of here soon," Mattheus said. "We'll go back to Grenada until we take the next case."

"I can't go," said Cindy.

"What are you talking about?" Mattheus flinched.

"Not without knowing who really killed Paul," Cindy said.

Mattheus breathed more easily and put his hand on Cindy's arm. "There are some things you never know," he spoke softly. "Some cases you never close. You have to learn to live with it, and move on."

"You haven't," Cindy said.

Mattheus smiled. "I'm trying to," he said.

Cindy knew that was true. She saw how hard he tried to keep going.

"But when hurricane season comes, when the storms hit," Mattheus continued, "you have to pack up and go."

"Not when there's an emergency," said Cindy.

"There's no emergency now," he said.

"An innocent woman put in jail isn't an emergency?"

"You don't know for sure that she's innocent."

"We don't know that she's not."

"You're stubborn as hell," Mattheus laughed.

"That's what keeps me going," said Cindy.

*

After their drinks Mattheus and Cindy each went to their rooms then, to wash up, relax, and prepare for dinner. Cindy sat down on her bed and looked up at the sky. It was heavy and overcast with threatening clouds. Mattheus was right. The storms would soon be coming. And the entire island was preparing for it—stores packing up, people getting out of town, stores selling batteries and jugs of water.

At dinner, Mattheus was quieter than usual. They'd had quite an afternoon, thought Cindy; he was probably just reflecting on it. Finally, as dessert was being served, he spoke up.

"I got two plane tickets for us back to Grenada for Wednesday." he said matter-of-factly.

Cindy was stunned. "I just said I didn't want to leave yet," she said.

"That's ridiculous. It doesn't make sense. There's nothing more we can do for her now."

"I disagree," said Cindy.

"Besides, she fired us," said Mattheus.

"She did it in a moment of upset," said Cindy. "It doesn't mean I'm running away. I don't care if she pays anymore. It's not all about money."

He leaned toward her powerfully. "It's dangerous to stay during a hurricane. If people don't have to be here, they're not."

"It's more dangerous to leave a case half cooked," said Cindy fitfully.

Mattheus grimaced. "Let's look at this realistically. Kendra's been caught lying over and over. She even lied to you."

"It doesn't mean she committed murder," said Cindy.

"It doesn't mean you can help her, either."

"Then what did she call us down here for?" asked Cindy.

"Maybe she thought you'd be easy to manipulate? Be part of a cover-up? Women like her often enjoy maneuvering other women."

Cindy took great exception to that. It made her feel like a child. "I'm not leaving the island until I'm sure," she said.

Mattheus stood up, annoyed. "Then it sounds like you'll be here alone for a very long time. Down here these things can take forever."

"Mattheus." Cindy reached up for him.

He looked down at her, as if from far away. "There's not one other viable suspect that's turned up. All loopholes have been covered. And I got a good deal on the plane tickets. We'll go back, take a break, and then pick up another case. There have been three articles about us already in the papers. I've had a couple of inquiries."

Cindy's body froze at the thought of leaving. She couldn't abandon Kendra like that.

"I'm just not ready," she said, "neither is the case. There's more to come, I feel it."

Mattheus shook his head. "Feelings can be tricky."

"I have to explore my hunches," Cindy insisted.

Mattheus was firm. "Look, I've seen this syndrome before and I don't want you getting caught in it. There are cops who are always looking for the next clue, chewing on a bare bone when all the meat's gone. They can't stand admitting failure and so they won't let go. If I thought there was any value at all in staying, don't you think I would?"

Mattheus' words hit Cindy hard. Was that what she was doing? Chewing on a bare bone? Living a life that had no juice in it? Mattheus was just trying to snap her out a trap he thought she was falling into. But she didn't feel finished.

"I'm staying," she said.

"Do what you want," snapped Mattheus, annoyed. "I'm getting out of here. There are intense storm warnings. It's scheduled to hit in a couple of days. The island people did their Hurricane Supplication Day festival early. You know what that is?"

"What?" asked Cindy, dumbfounded.

"It's a holiday when the locals ask to be spared from devastating storms. They're expecting category four winds—135-mile force. You have to be out of your mind to stay down here."

Mattheus could say what he liked. Cindy knew she couldn't leave.

They left the restaurant together without saying a word. Once out in the lobby, instead of going back up to her room, Cindy turned and walked out of the hotel. She refused to be pressured by Mattheus and couldn't help thinking about Nell, left alone without her father and her mother now in jail. Cindy had been shocked to see Nell arrive at the lunch. Clearly, she'd wanted to meet Margot. Nell had mentioned at the time that she thought Margot did it. Cindy had let that comment just lie there, but she'd been wondering about it more these days. She wanted to talk with Nell about it. Cindy never felt that she'd spent enough time with her. At the very least she could visit, say hello, and give her some support and comfort.

Cindy hailed a cab and decided to take it straight to Kendra's home. It was windy and cooler than usual, and the rain kept falling harder, making the roads slippery and slick. Mattheus was probably at the bar, alone, talking to whoever was around. She couldn't let herself think about him. He was wrong to pressure her in that way. If they were going to be a team, they'd have to make decisions together. Since when was he scared of a storm?

The drive to Kendra's house went quickly and when Cindy arrived, strangely enough, the front door was open. Cindy turned the knob and walked in. The place felt silent, empty and haunted, filled with desolation and gloom. For a second, Cindy felt scared, as if something worse were hovering.

She walked around the downstairs slowly, looking in corners, wondering where Nell was. Maybe visiting her mother in jail. But, maybe not? Cindy thought of calling out for her, but decided instead to go upstairs and see if she might be in her room.

She got to the second floor and behind one door heard a strange hum. Cindy knocked on the door. No one answered. Before she opened it, she decided to knock again.

"What the hell do you want?" a raw voice called from inside.

Cindy jumped back, startled, "It's Cindy Blaine, can I come in?"

Even before she finished saying that, the door flung open and Nell stood there, staring.

"What are you doing here?" The words poured out of her by themselves. "Who let you in?"

"The door was open," Cindy said. "I'm sorry."

"You can be as sorry as you want, but what did you really do for us? Nothing. My mom's locked up and my father's dead."

Cindy bit her lip. "I'm not done yet," she said strongly. "Help me to help you, please."

Nell laughed a loud coarse laugh, and tossed her wild hair off her face.

"Can I come into your room?" Cindy asked. She wanted to look around, sit down, and have some time for the two of them together.

Nell flung the door to the room open wider. "What the hell do I care? Come in."

Cindy walked in after her. The room was a total wreck. Clothes were strewn on the floor, paintings on the wall were taken down or hanging at weird angles. Her laptop was open on the floor in the middle of all of it.

"What happened here?" Cindy asked, alarmed.

"Nothing," said Nell, grinning now, showing a row of small, perfect teeth. "This is how I live. You got a problem with it?"

"No," Cindy said. "I'm just frightened for you."

"Don't be," said Nell. "The time for worrying about me is long gone."

Cindy walked in farther and sat on a small chair.

Nell pulled up a broken chair and sat down opposite her. For a moment she seemed glad to have Cindy around.

"This has to be hell for you," Cindy started. "First your father and now your mom."

"Hell's putting it mildly," Nell said

"I know you and your father were close." Cindy wanted more from her, craved it, sensed the heart of what happened was right here.

"My father was a dick," said Nell quietly.

Cindy was shocked. But it was natural that Nell should feel that way after she'd found out that her father had been married to someone else.

"Because of the other wife?" asked Cindy.

Nell's face puckered. "No. Who cared if he had another wife? I couldn't blame him for that, one bit. My mother's a bitch. She was always a bitch—to both of us. I'm not saying she killed him, I don't think she did. Just that she was a bitch. If my father had half a brain he would have stayed there with his other wife. But he couldn't. He kept running home."

Cindy looked around the turbulent room. Parts of it looked like any high school kid's room, posters of rock stars and papers strewn around. She wanted to see what was on Nell's computer and leaned down toward it.

"Just talking to my friends on Facebook," said Nell.

"I'm sure you have a lot of them," said Cindy. "Mind if I take a look?"

"Look all you want," said Nell as Cindy picked the laptop up.

It was open to Nell's homepage. Cindy started looking at the people and then stopped cold. Her heart started beating wildly. Right on the top was a photo of Nell and Graham.

"Who's this?" she asked Nell, totally shocked.

"Graham Kowan," said Nell matter-of-factly. "Why?"

Cindy turned toward Nell, amazed. "You knew Graham Kowan? Your father's son?"

Nell just stared at the photos and said nothing.

Cindy reached out to her. "You've got to tell me about this, Nell."

"There's nothing to tell," Nell murmured.

"You and Graham were friends?" Cindy pursued it.

Nell remained silent.

“How did you know him?” Cindy was speechless.

Nell became sullen. “He goes to my school,” she said, “no big deal.”

“You knew about your father’s second family for a long time?”

Nell shook her head. “No.” Flames darted from her eyes.

“Nell, you’ve got to talk to me about this.” Cindy could barely catch her breath. Her mind was racing. She needed to know about this relationship, how it started and why.

But Nell had enough. She pulled her scraggly sweater close around her, went to her door, and opened it up. “Go home now. I’m tired,” she said to Cindy. “It’s enough.”

A wave of sorrow flooded Cindy, leaving Nell alone there.

“You can trust me, Nell,” Cindy said softly.

A distorted look crept over Nell’s face. “Oh yeah, I can trust you. Fat chance. Go home now,” she demanded.

*

All the way home in the cab Cindy watched the heavy rain fall, blurring her vision so that, looking through the side windows, the road disappeared from view. Cindy could not erase the image of Nell and Graham from her mind. The two of them looked oddly at one, unlikely partners who had no right to meet, much less to connect. Cindy wondered whether she should tell Mattheus about this development, but decided not to. It was too premature. She had no real idea what all of this meant, or where it might possibly lead. Cindy decided to go to see Kendra in jail first thing the next morning and talk to her about it.

Usually, when Cindy returned to the hotel and walked into the lobby, Mattheus was there waiting for her. This time he wasn’t. Maybe he was up in his room? She went to the desk to call him. As she dialed she heard the television in the hotel lobby speaking about the oncoming storm. Flights off the island were packed full, ports would soon be closed. The phone to Mattheus’ room just rang and rang. Cindy’s heart dropped.

“Did you see happen to see Mattheus King?” she asked the man at the desk.

“Checked out,” he said.

Cindy felt her body turn cold. It wasn’t possible.

“Lots of visitors leaving. You heard the warnings about Lola? Going to hit St. Thomas real soon.”

Mattheus meant what he said, thought Cindy. He was letting a little storm run him out of town. Cindy took a deep breath. This was totally shocking. He had told her he was leaving, but she hadn't believed him for a second. Couldn't imagine he'd leave her alone here with the case. Clint would never have done this. He'd stay at her side through thick and thin. Well, now I know what this person is made of, Cindy said to herself. Better find out sooner than later. But deep within she felt lonely and scared.

"Hey," the guy behind the desk said, "you staying around during the storm?"

"Yes," said Cindy.

"There's gonna be a shelter about a mile from here to go when the electricity shuts down. They're collecting jugs of water, batteries, bread, juice, and canned food. This isn't the best place to be. It's low ground. When those winds hit, the roofs go flying."

"I'll be fine," said Cindy.

"Don't be so sure," the guy said, "I've seen the storm wipe away stronger folks than you. If you want to stay alive, you better watch out."

CHAPTER 22

When Cindy awoke the next morning the clouds had grown thicker and the winds picked up. She immediately turned on the TV in her room.

"Hurricane Lola is bringing gusty winds, rain, and generally foul weather to St. Thomas," the reporter said. "As the storm intensifies throughout the day, both of the territory's airports will be closed, seaports shut. Expect power outages to hit and shelters to be opened on St. Thomas, St. Croix, and St. John. The governor has declared a state of emergency, imposing a curfew from six p.m. this evening to 6 a.m. tomorrow. The U.S. Coast Guard has closed the ports until further notice. Emergency shelters will be open at St. Croix Educational Complex and at the Sugar Estate Head Start Center on St. Thomas."

Cindy was riveted to the TV.

"The biggest concern," the commentator continued, "is the wind and rain. We've already had a significant amount of rainfall and the ground is just about saturated. More rainfall could cause downed trees, mudslides, and rockslides. Waste Management is also concerned about overflows in sewer collection. Avoid known areas where manhole overflows occur and proceed through standing water with extreme caution!"

As the commentator went on and on, Cindy called down to order breakfast in her room.

She didn't need to have breakfast with Mattheus downstairs, as they usually did. A new kind of power filled Cindy. It felt good being independent, coming and going as she pleased. She could handle the storm and also the case, with or without Mattheus. She'd prefer to do it with him, but only if things were mutual. An odd kind of strength filled her at that realization, and a freedom she relished as well.

The storm hadn't hit yet and the curfew wasn't until 6 p.m. She'd ride it out at the hotel or at the shelter nearby.

The bell boy brought breakfast and Cindy finished it, turned off the TV, and went downstairs. She knew she had to see Kendra again before the storm hit. Had to ask her about Nell and Graham.

Even though she'd been fired, the case had taken on a life of its own, much like the storm that was coming.

CHAPTER 23

The local airport was filled to capacity. Mattheus was crunched with others, waiting to get off the island. He'd checked his luggage and headed here, eager to get back to Grenada. Outside, the winds blew fiercely. He hoped they could take off before it got worse.

It was definitely crazy that Cindy wasn't with him, but she wouldn't listen to sense. And he wasn't into forcing anyone. It made him feel stupid and small. The case was over, Kendra was in jail, and beyond that, they'd both been fired. Mattheus hadn't been able to see one sane reason for staying on the island and putting himself in danger. At first he'd been sure that Cindy would come to her senses. But he hadn't heard a word from her as storm warnings increased.

Right now he'd been waiting in line for over an hour. It would be a few minutes before the flight boarded. Mattheus wondered what Cindy was doing back there, where she'd ride the storm out. She had no idea how hard it would be, either. Mattheus realized that. She was idealistic, but also pig-headed. If this was what she wanted, let her have it.

Mattheus' flight was now being called to board. He grabbed his overnight bag and quickly went to the gate. He couldn't wait to get off the island, back to the calm, beautiful world he'd grown to love.

He showed his ticket, walked onto the plane, and packed his bag safely overhead. This was one of the last planes out before the storm and he was damned lucky to have a seat on it. He took his aisle seat and waited while others were boarding. There was a sense of urgency as the plane filled up, and Mattheus was hit with a wave of anxiety. How the hell was Cindy going to manage alone? The thought of her there in the huge winds and rain suddenly made him feel like throwing up.

He put his head back on the seat and tried to block her out of his mind. He couldn't. She'd chosen this, he thought. He'd gotten plane tickets for both of them, tried his best to reason with her. No matter what he told himself, the anxiety gnawed. Damn, he thought, he couldn't do it. He had to get back to the hotel as fast as he could to be there with her when the storm hit.

Mattheus jumped out of the seat, grabbed his bag, and pushed through the crowded aisle, back to the plane's entrance. Then he flew down the plank, out into the airport, and rushed for all he was worth to grab a taxi before it was too late.

CHAPTER 24

Cindy hailed a cab and took it to the jailhouse. As it drove along the streets, she saw the streets were much emptier, but there were also people left, rushing back and forth with packages, boarding up their houses. There was a strange excitement being a part of the fierce energy the storm was bringing.

The jailhouse, located farther out on the island, was small and low, and half empty, as this was the women's division. The winds hadn't hit this part of the island yet, and there was an odd calm hovering about it.

Cindy had to wait for the officials to bring Kendra to her. They put her in the waiting room, which had wood plank floors, two wooden benches, and a photo of a bird on the wall. On the far corner was a table with paper coffee cups and a pot of coffee. A large female guard with big hips walked in and out of the waiting room from time to time.

Cindy got up, poured herself some coffee, and added a nice, heaping serving of sugar.

The woman watched her as she stirred it all together. "What's someone like you doing at a place like this?" the woman finally asked, curiosity getting the better of her.

Cindy turned and looked at her. "I'm a private detective," she said.

The woman threw her head back and guffawed. "You? You're making me split my sides laughing."

Her laugh was contagious. Cindy couldn't help but smile. "What's so funny about that?" she asked.

"Nothing, honey, but it's the last thing in the world you look like," the woman said. "I thought you were one of her daughters. You look so young. And innocent."

Cindy never thought of herself as innocent. "Just new to the game."

The woman laughed again. "Well, you never know—it does take brains."

Takes more than that, thought Cindy. "Takes heart," she said.

"And a tough skin," the woman added. "Better not forget that. These inmates know what they're doing. They're one slippery bunch. Can get one over on anyone. Used to fool me plenty in the beginning. Now I can see through them the second they come in."

Cindy could believe that. This woman seemed as planted as a huge tree, with roots that sank down deep into the middle of the earth.

"You know what you're doing staying for the storm?" The woman looked at Cindy closely.

"Sure," said Cindy. "I've got important work to do."

Kendra, dressed in orange overalls, was brought into the waiting room, accompanied by a female officer.

"You have a maximum of twenty minutes together," the officer announced. Clearly it was official policy and she was informing Cindy of it. That will be more than enough, Cindy thought, as the officer departed.

"What are you doing here?" Kendra looked startled, seeing Cindy. "You've been fired."

"I'm working the case anyway," said Cindy. "I'm not done."

"I'm not paying you anything."

"There's more at stake than money," said Cindy. "I never give up on anybody."

Kendra was taken aback.

"I want to find the killer," said Cindy.

Kendra looked surprised. "You don't mean you don't actually believe I killed Paul?"

"I have my doubts," said Cindy.

"Only doubts?"

"I still have questions."

"Okay, shoot, what are they?" Kendra seemed ready to answer anything now.

"Tell me about Nell and Graham," Cindy said immediately.

Kendra seemed momentarily confused. "You mean Graham Kowan? Paul's son?"

"Yes—his relationship with Nell?"

Kendra's brow furrowed. "Nell and Graham?" She sounded stunned.

"I saw a photo of them together," said Cindy. You've never seen it?" Cindy focused in on her for all she was worth.

"Never." Kendra was shocked. "Where did you see it? Why was it taken?"

"Listen, Kendra"—Cindy was annoyed—"if you're not honest with me now, I can't help you."

"I'm telling you the truth," Kendra said. "I never saw any photos. I had no idea they knew each other. Don't you think I'd tell you if I knew? How did you even see those pictures?"

"I went to your house last night," said Cindy. "Nell was there. I went into her room to talk. I saw them on her Facebook page."

Kendra's mouth hung open as she listened. "Believe me, I had no idea she ever met Graham at all."

"How is that possible?" said Cindy.

"Nell and I aren't close. She doesn't tell me anything. She hasn't even been here to visit me once," said Kendra.

"I can understand why," said Cindy, bitterly.

"Why?" Kendra's eyes flared.

"She's going through hell."

"Nell's always going through one hell or another." Kendra voice grew harsh. "The truth is she can't stand me, never could, not even when she was a little girl. I told you before, she preferred her father. For some reason I never understood, he adored her. Whenever he was home, she was the one he'd spend his time with."

"You couldn't have liked that very much," said Cindy.

"In the beginning I didn't," said Kendra, the muscles in her face trembling. "But I got used to it. You get used to all kinds of things as time passes."

"Like your husband having a second family?" Cindy had to dig at her. Kendra was ready now to talk. She had no reason not to. There was no way out of here for her if she didn't.

"Not that," said Kendra. "I got used to him having a relationship with Heather. That only went on for a few years. Heather was different from me. A side dish. I could deal with it."

"But a second family?" Cindy wasn't letting go. "He must have been gone so much. You deserved better."

"I had what I needed," Kendra said flippantly.

"That's not how it looks to others," said Cindy.

"What difference does it make how it looks? Everyone's made up their mind. They decided I did it the first day Paul was found. Book closed. Case completed."

Kendra got up from the bench and walked to the small windows that lined the room. It was dark out and the winds were starting. "Storm is coming soon," she said.

"You'll be safe here," said Cindy.

"I'm not safe anywhere, anymore," Kendra said.

Cindy came up beside her. "How long did you know about his other family?" she asked. She needed more and more details, couldn't help feeling that somewhere, buried in the center of this morass, one unexpected memory would untie the entire web.

"What makes you say I knew about them?" asked Kendra, trembling.

"Don't play games with me!" Cindy was on edge. "This is your last chance to get free."

"If I knew that Paul had two families"—Kendra cringed—"that would only make it look worse for me."

"Not necessarily," said Cindy. "Tell me the entire truth. One fact leads to another. You'll set me on the right trail."

"I knew about them for the past seven years," Kendra finally whispered.

Cindy stopped breathing. "How did you find out?"

"It happened strangely. One day I saw a snapshot on the floor of Paul and a boy of about eleven, Graham. The boy was clinging onto his father. I looked and looked at it for a long time, thought the photo must have fallen out of Paul's pocket."

Cindy took a long, slow breath. "Awful!"

"Not really," said Kendra. "It was actually fascinating. This child looked exactly like Paul's brother, who had died when he was young. The minute I saw the photo, I knew this child was Paul's son. So, I thought it was a love child. I had no idea that he'd actually married the mother. But it was fantastic to find the photograph. Proof of something you knew all along deep down, but couldn't put your finger on and makes you feel like you're crazy."

That was exactly the way Cindy felt about this case.

"I showed Paul the photo a few days later, before he was about to leave on his usual trip. He stared at it, horrified. Then he stared at me. At first he tried to lie, said it was some kid from a charity he was working with. That didn't go over with me for a minute. I slapped him hard, in the face." Kendra smiled now, thinking of it. "He needed that slap, he deserved it."

Cindy felt chilled. What else had she done to Paul over the years to make him pay for this?

"Paul got scared. For a minute he was going to slap me back, but then he looked in my eyes. What did he see? I often wonder. Maybe he saw that I didn't care.

"I just need the truth," I told him. 'The kid's my son,' he said, terrified.

"You know, Paul was a tremendously weak man. Despite his grand life and big cover, underneath he lived like a crazy person and was terrified of being found out. And he was also very rich.

Whatever he touched brought him big money. It made him think he could rule the world, do whatever he liked."

"You stayed with him because of the money?" Cindy zeroed in.

"No," said Kendra, "definitely not. I had an income of my own. I could have built my tour business any time I wanted. Look, at first I just thought he had a kid with someone else, I had no idea he was married. I'm not saying that wasn't rotten—"

"Why did you stay?"

Kendra turned and walked away from the window and began slowly pacing back and forth.

"I'm as weak as he was," she said, looking down at the floor.

Cindy walked beside her. "He had something on you?"

Kendra laughed out loud. "Of course not. What could he have? I'm weak because I was also frightened."

"Afraid of who?"

"Of Nell," she said. "Afraid of raising her alone. I couldn't bear the thought of it. It would have been far too much for me. So I stayed. But it haunted me. I searched further and found out about Margot, the wife.

"When I told him about it, Paul didn't deny any of it. He just said Margot had no idea about me or Nell—and that he had no intention of telling her. He felt indebted to the bitch for everything. She gave him all the money he needed to get going in life—paid for law school, set up his office, paid for their home, and ours too. Who knew? He said he married her out of obligation and then a year later, met me—and really fell in love. He didn't want to lose me ever, so he decided to marry me, too. He actually started crying when he said that. I told him to stop his blubbering. He looked at me with sick fish eyes. He said that Margot and I were pregnant at the same time. Graham was born a few months before I had Nell. He couldn't get out of either marriage."

"You lived with this for seven years?" said Cindy.

"You get used to all kinds of things," said Kendra. "In the meantime I did my thing and he did his. There were other people I was with. I figured I'd get out when Nell was grown. I knew where I stood. I had the truth. That's a lot more than most women have."

"Go on," said Cindy intensely.

"I didn't ask him anything more about his son, Graham. I knew that he went to high school on the mainland, but I didn't care. That's where he and Nell must have met."

Cindy and Kendra then stared at each other and a chill went through both of them at the same time.

“I never knew Nell and Graham were friends,” Kendra said in a plaintive tone. “There was no way Nell could have known who he was either.”

Kendra wove a fantastic web and Cindy was fascinated. She wondered, though, as Kendra spoke whether she could believe any of it. Her moments of hatred toward Paul were laser sharp. It made sense that Kendra would finally get fed up with him and put an end to all of it.

“Why didn’t you tell me this before?” Cindy breathed.

“What difference does it make if I knew about his other marriage or not?” asked Kendra. “It’s just sordid family history. It has nothing to do with who killed him.”

“That’s ridiculous,” said Cindy. “Everything has something to do with who might have killed him. How do you know that Margot didn’t find out and do it?”

Kendra smirked. “I heard about her for so many years. She couldn’t live without Paul, wrapped her life around him. She was a spineless creature, living in a dream world. There would have been no way for her to do it. If she did find out, she’d simply fall apart. That was her main tactic with him when things didn’t go well, or when he spent too much time away.”

“Can you see why people think you did it?” Cindy asked pointedly.

“I see,” said Kendra tartly. “But I didn’t do it. And that’s the truth.”

The time had fled much more quickly than Cindy realized. When she looked up she suddenly saw the female police officer coming to get Kendra.

“It can’t be that twenty minutes have passed,” said Cindy.

“Find out who did it,” she called out desperately, as the police officer grabbed her arm and yanked her out the door.

CHAPTER 25

Cindy stood outside alone waiting for the taxi to come get her and take her back to the hotel. It was hard not to have Mattheus nearby, to call him and tell him what she'd found out. And it was hard to believe he was on a plane, leaving without her. She didn't have to believe it, though. In a few seconds her phone rang.

"You there?" It was Mattheus' voice, sounding urgent.

"Mattheus? I thought you'd checked out, were on your way back to Grenada."

"I checked out and now I've checked back in again," said Mattheus in a gruff tone.

"Cindy's heart lifted. "Why?"

"Forget the whys. Where are you?" he asked, irritated.

"At the jailhouse," she said.

"Good God," he said, "you didn't tell me you were going there."

"How could I tell you? You weren't here."

"Well, I'm here now, and thank God I am. I checked back in with the police as soon as I returned and I have news for you."

Cindy's heart started pounding. "I'll be back at the hotel in half an hour," said Cindy.

"Before you go anywhere, listen to me," Mattheus said. "There's a break in the case! Get ready."

"What?" asked Cindy, shaken.

"Graham has been found dead!"

CHAPTER 26

When Cindy's taxi pulled up, Margot's house was roped off as a crime scene, with rows of police cars lined up in front. Photographers, on the edges of the property, were snapping pictures for the paper, as heavy rain fell on all of them.

Cindy got out of the taxi and saw Mattheus a few feet away, looking down the road, waiting for her. He immediately ran over with a big, black opened umbrella. Cindy got under the umbrella with him and they wound their way through the crowd of cops. Fortunately, Mattheus had clearance for them to get in.

"Unbelievable," Cindy breathed, as they approached the front door.

"Worse than that," said Mattheus, his arm now tight around her.

"What?" asked Cindy, horrified. "Margot?"

"Can you imagine?" said Mattheus. "Right now she's on heavy sedation. They were afraid she'd have a heart attack when she found out."

"Was she the one who found Graham?"

"Yeah," said Mattheus. "A complete nightmare."

Cindy shivered and moved closer to him in the pouring rain.

They got to the door, and Mattheus opened it, shook out the umbrella, and the two of them walked in. Everything in the house seemed the same, perfectly organized, not a paper out of place. Only the wind whipping at the shuttered windows gave any indication that something was wrong.

"He's still upstairs in his room," Mattheus said. "I've seen the body."

Cindy hadn't yet seen a dead body—and didn't want to.

"You don't have to actually go up and look at it," said Mattheus. "We have clearance to go, and it can be helpful. You could notice something."

"I'll go," said Cindy.

Trembling, she walked up the stairs with Mattheus to Graham's room, stood at the edge of it, and looked in. He was still there, lying silently on the floor, trickles of blood around his neck. He looked fantastically still, oddly at peace.

Cindy wanted to take him in her arms and hug him, tell him it was all a bad dream, and that he should come back to life. He was so young, had so many years before him. She thought of the beautiful pictures of him and Nell. He'd seemed so happy in them. There were a few cops inside, dusting for prints, walking around the body gingerly.

"Another stabbing." A cop came up behind them.

"Why?" asked Cindy, not noticing who he was.

"Same way the father was killed?" said Mattheus.

"Could be." The cop came and stood beside them. It was Nojo. He seemed sad, quieter. This had sobered him up. It stunned and sobered everybody.

"We only got maybes at this point," Nojo said.

"Kendra was in jail when this happened," Cindy remarked slowly.

"Yes, she was," said Nojo, shaking his head.

"Who was here in the house?" Cindy turned and looked at him directly.

"Only the mother," he said, quietly. Clearly, this had taken them all off guard. Suddenly Kendra might not be the main suspect any longer—and Cindy wasn't the enemy who'd flown into town to help someone they all hated.

"Where exactly is Margot now?" asked Cindy.

"Off limits. In her room with doctors," Nojo said. "She's hysterical. But, as far as we can tell, she was the only one within miles of this kid today. And with the storms like they are, nobody was traveling."

Mattheus let out a long breath. "Sweet Jesus," he said.

"Ain't always so sweet." Nojo jostled him. "You know that."

Cindy just stared at Graham, who looked defenseless lying there alone. She couldn't put it together, see the point in his death.

"Let's hope he's with his father now," Nojo said quietly.

Cindy suddenly felt agitated. They should have seen something like this coming—been prepared. How could it have hit them from behind? They'd all missed something important and it led to a senseless death.

"Who called this in?" she asked.

"The mother," said Nojo. "We couldn't make out what she was saying for a long, long time. She just kept yelling, come over, come over. Then we came and found this."

"No one's talked to her yet?" asked Cindy.

Both Mattheus and Nojo looked at her strangely.

"It's way too soon," said Mattheus.

"She can't talk," Nojo said. "That doesn't mean she's not a suspect. What else in the hell can we make of it? She could have gone crazy after finding out about the second wife. Could be the lunch was too much for her. Could be she snapped. Maybe the son suddenly reminded her of the husband. Then she forgot herself for a few seconds. That's all it takes. A few seconds of rage, revenge, and before you know it, someone is dead. Sometimes the one who did it doesn't even realize they did. It's like a flash fire that burns out of nowhere and then goes out. Are they guilty then? It's a big question."

Cindy turned to walk away.

"Hey, don't take it so hard," Nojo said to her, reaching out to bring her back. "We'll find the killer, they got lots of prints here."

Cindy nodded sadly. "Well, at least it isn't Kendra," she said.

"Nope," Nojo agreed, "she definitely didn't do *this*. But we have no idea if the two killings are tied to each other yet."

"Oh, come on now," said Cindy.

"Looks like it," Nojo had to agree, "but for now, no one's sure."

CHAPTER 27

There was no reason to stay here much longer. Margot was out of commission and the place was crawling with police and detectives searching for evidence. But Cindy had a clue no one else ever dreamt of—the photo she'd seen of Graham and Nell. She couldn't get it out of her mind. Their faces shone out at her, pressuring her to dig deeper. She had to get out of here immediately and go speak with Nell.

"I've got something no one knows about yet," Cindy finally said urgently to Mattheus. "There's someone I've got to talk to immediately."

Mattheus was taken aback. "Who?" he asked.

"Come with me to the mainland and I'll tell you on in the car."

Mattheus hesitated. The action was here.

Cindy knew it seemed crazy to leave the scene of a crime. "If you'd rather stay here, it's fine," said Cindy. "I'll call for a taxi and go back myself. Then we'll talk later when you return."

Once again, Mattheus hesitated. "Are you in any danger doing this alone?"

Cindy appreciated that.

"Do you need me with you back there? The storm isn't due to hit for another few hours."

Cindy smiled. It felt good having the old Mattheus back. She felt cared for and appreciated. She didn't need him to actually go with her; it was enough that he cared.

"Not at all," she said. "It's fine for the two of us to cover different fronts."

Mattheus looked at her appreciatively. "Good. We'll make best use of our time that way." Then his eyes crinkled into a little smile for a moment, "And, our little spat is over?" he asked.

"Completely." Cindy smiled. "You came back." It was huge for him and Cindy realized it.

The taxi pulled off and Mattheus dissolved into a blur of rain. It was best this way, thought Cindy, she needed to speak to Nell alone. The story would hit the papers tomorrow; there was no way Nell could have heard yet. Cindy didn't want her to be alone when she found out the news.

The drive was shaky in the winds and rain and seemed to take forever. Cindy had plenty of time to think everything over. There had to be a connection between the two murders, first a father, then a son. Kendra was locked up when this murder took place. This would have to create questions about her guilt. Would Margot now become a suspect? Cindy found it hard to imagine how Margot could have taken her own son's life. Or her husband's, either, for that matter. But Cindy knew she had to keep every possibility open. As soon as you closed your mind, the case was shut down.

When the taxi finally pulled up at Kendra's home, Cindy got out and rushed to the front door. No answer. The door was open, though, and Cindy walked in, closed the umbrella, and shook off the rain from her clothing. It was empty and silent again inside, but schools were closed for the storm. Cindy knew Nell had to be home. Rather than going right up to Nell's room, Cindy called her name, on the chance that she could hear her, and would not be taken by surprise.

"Nell," Cindy called, her voice echoing through the empty rooms.

No answer.

"Nell, it's Cindy, are you home?"

More silence. Cindy decided to climb the stairs and knock on Nell's door. If she wasn't there, at the very least, Cindy could spend more time on her computer.

Cindy knocked on Nell's door, softly at first, then louder. No answer at all. She turned the knob and walked in the room. Nell was on the floor in the corner, curled up.

Cindy was horrified. "Nell?"

Nell didn't move or look up.

Cindy went over, bent down, and put her hands on Nell's shoulders. "Are you all right?" Cindy said.

Nell grunted like a wounded animal.

She must have found out about Graham, Cindy thought. "Look at me, Nell," Cindy said as softly as she could manage.

Very slowly, Nell looked up through unfocused eyes that were bloodshot.

"It's going to be all right." Cindy tried to hug her, but Nell lurched away.

"Don't touch me," she muttered. "Nothing's gonna be all right."

"You heard what happened?" Cindy asked gently.

Nell threw her head back and laughed. "Of course I heard."

Cindy was startled. "When did you find out?" she asked.

Nell laughed again, a loud, rough, raucous sound.

Cindy knew that shock manifested in all kinds of ways. Obviously, she had found out that Graham was dead. Cindy had to find out how. "Tell me how you heard the news," Cindy demanded.

"What news?" Nell said, bleary.

Cindy put her hands on Nell's shoulders and gave her a shake. She had to break the spell Nell was under. "You've got to calm down and talk to me, Nell."

"And what if I don't?" Nell's eyes suddenly flashed and her tone turned sharp and bitter.

"How did you find out that Graham was dead?"

"An angel told me," said Nell, and she laughed again.

Cindy shook her harder. "This isn't a game. We have to find out who did it. The killer could strike again."

That stopped Nell for a moment. Then she sprang up and shook herself off. "Graham's dead. He's dead," she started shrieking.

Cindy held Nell's face in her hands. "Stop this!" she yelled back.

Nell started crying. "You can't tell me he isn't dead. I heard it with my own ears."

Cindy shuddered tremendously. "How?"

"A friend told me," Nell yelped.

"What friend?" Cindy started closing in. "You have to tell me. You cared about Graham. The two of you were good friends."

"We weren't good friends, we loved each other. We were boyfriend and girlfriend."

Cindy's head started to swim. She'd thought that when she'd looked at the photos, but it was different hearing it from Nell.

"You saw that he loved me on the photos." The words were now pouring out of Nell. "Don't play your stupid head games with me."

"I'm not playing any games." Cindy's voice got louder as she tried to absorb what Nell was saying. "I want to help you. I want to help your mother."

"It's too late for that," said Nell.

"It's never too late."

"Go to hell." Nell almost spit in Cindy's face.

Cindy put her arm up to block her face, and moved in closer. "Did your mother know about you and Graham?"

"My mother didn't know anything. She didn't care either. She didn't know who any of my friends were. But my father knew!"

"Your father?" Cindy was stunned.

"One day, when Graham was here, my father came home early from a trip! He came up to my room to say hello, and he saw him."

Cindy went on high alert.

Nell started talking faster now, unable to stop. "I didn't think anything about it. Why should I? So I had a boyfriend, so what? But my father's face got white the minute he saw Graham. He looked like he was in shock. Graham and I looked at each other. We had no idea what was going on. My father's eyes narrowed in a way I'd never seen before. He looked at Graham as if he'd seen a ghost. Graham and I got more and more frightened. Then my father suddenly starting shouting so loud, we started shaking. How did you find out about Nell? my father kept asking him. Graham didn't know what he was talking about. He thought his father had come to visit. Find out what? he yelled back."

Cindy's heart started pounding.

"Once in a while, I'd seen my father in rages like that. But not too often," Nell continued, the words tripping faster and faster over each other. "When my father started yelling at us, I thought it was because he was jealous."

"It was more than that though." Cindy urged her onwards.

"You can say that again." Nell bit her lip so hard Cindy thought it would start to bleed. "Much more. All of a sudden my father started yelling that we were half brother and sister. He yelled it so loud I thought a vein in his neck would bust and he'd drop dead of a stroke on the spot. Too bad he didn't! It would have saved us a lot of misery and pain."

"Half brother and sister," Cindy repeated. "Did you believe him?"

"Of course not," Nell whimpered, "not in the beginning. I thought my dad hooked up with someone and imagined that Graham was his child. I thought he'd finally gone nuts. He was always nuts around the edges."

Little beads of perspiration broke out on Cindy's forehead. She felt a mixture of incredible pity and terror for Nell.

"What happened to Graham?" Cindy asked then straightforwardly. Nell was on a roll. Cindy felt she would answer any question that was put to her now. She couldn't stop.

"Things got too complicated," Nell continued, a fierce pressure under her words. She seemed almost relieved to be talking. "It took Graham awhile to realize that he and I had the same father. When he did, Graham went nuts. His relationship with my father changed overnight. My father insisted Graham stop seeing me. Graham refused. He was crazy about me. He became enraged at the suggestion. His relationship with me changed too. He began calling all day long, coming over at strange times. It terrified me. He said he'd never let go, never listen to his father."

"Did your father tell you that he had two wives, was married to both your mothers?"

"Finally, he told us. That made it worse for Graham, made him hate my father more. I didn't know what to believe. It was a shock to think that my dad had two wives. I used to look at my mother and think what an idiot he was making of her. I didn't care so much about that, though. She wasn't good to him, ever. She never really loved him, I didn't think it would matter to her. But when Graham realized that my father really had two wives, it was terrible for him. I'm not allowed to have anyone, Graham would say over and over, and Dad can have whoever he wants?

"One night it was too much. They had a terrible fight. I was there when it happened. My father told us both to meet him for dinner, at the mall, behind a back alley. We went, sat there opposite him while he tapped his fingers on the table hard. You two are bringing a curse on the whole family, he said. Imagine him talking about a curse, a man married to two women at once. It really made Graham nuts. He couldn't stand it. It was the last straw.

"My father went on and on and then, suddenly, Graham just flipped out. He jumped up, grabbed the steak knife, and lurched over toward my dad. I grabbed Graham's wrist, twisted his hand, and the knife fell back down on the table. My father looked like he was going to explode. He started to call Graham rotten and smarmy.

"Like father, like son, Graham yelled as his face contorted. You cheating on two women at once. Be a man, stand up and tell the truth.

"My father jumped out of his seat and ran out the back of the restaurant. Graham wasn't going to let him go. He grabbed the knife and ran out after him to the narrow side street. It was just getting dark. The street was empty. I ran behind both of them, but when I got there, it was too late. Graham had caught my dad by the back of the neck and started stabbing. There was blood pouring all over. I screamed and screamed but nothing came out. My voice was frozen.

"Finally, Graham dumped my dad on the ground. I was terrified. Graham started running, but I couldn't leave my dad alone like that. I ran into the restaurant for help, then stopped. Who would believe me? No one." Nell's eyes were clear now and gleaming.

"Did you catch up with him?"

"No. He was gone. I didn't know where he went. I just knew that he took the knife with him. I went running back to the alleyway, to my dad. He was laying there uncovered. I threw leaves and branches over him to cover him up. Later on, a few people walked by. They didn't even notice. I even grabbed a piece of paper that was lying on the floor and scrawled a good-bye note on it. Then I stuck it in the wall."

That must have been the note Cindy'd found.

"Your mother's in jail for the crime," Cindy said, breathless. "They've been suspecting her all along."

"There was no way I was going to tell on Graham." Nell was babbling. "How could I? I loved him. And it wasn't his fault. My father asked for it, he pushed both of us right up to the edge."

"Now Graham's dead too," Cindy said, pointedly, reining her in. "Who killed him?"

Nell looked up at her, scared. "Graham couldn't live with himself after this happened. He got more and more agitated every day, had to see me constantly to tell him it was okay. It was too much for me, I couldn't take it. He was making me crazy. Can you understand that?"

"Yes, I can," said Cindy.

"I told him to give me some time, to stay away. He wouldn't listen. No matter what I said, the next minute he'd call. I didn't know what to do. I couldn't get a minute's peace. I couldn't sleep at night anymore."

Cindy felt a long chill go up and down her back.

"So I called a tough kid in school I know. This kid likes me. He's tough, but he's sweet. He wouldn't hurt anyone. I told him Graham was bothering me and I couldn't take it anymore. I asked him to keep Graham away, to frighten him off a little bit. That's all I said. I thought he'd rough him up a little and that would be that." Nell started gasping for air. "I never wanted to hurt him. The kid didn't mean to hurt him. They fought, they wrestled. Things went wrong."

Nell's face was pouring with perspiration as tears started to fall. She shot up and went for the bureau drawer, pulled it open, and yanked out a big, glistening, silver knife.

"Is that the knife Graham used to kill your father?" Cindy asked, horrified.

"Yes," Nell yelled, now holding it up to her own throat. "And I'm killing myself with it. I don't want to live anymore."

"Nell, give that to me," Cindy yelled back. "You can't do it. It wasn't your fault."

"It was my fault. I deserve it. I want to die."

As Nell raised the knife high, Cindy flew at her, yanked the knife out of her hand, and held her tightly as Nell sobbed and sobbed so loudly, it drowned out the winds, the pounding rain, and the wooden shutters that were banging madly against the walls.

CHAPTER 28

YOUNG WOMAN DETECTIVE SOLVES SORDID MURDER ON HER OWN!

Once again the headlines screamed the news of Cindy's victory in the strange, convoluted case. Mattheus bought at least ten copies, grinning from ear to ear.

"You have an angel with you, whispering secrets none of us can hear."

Cindy smiled wanly. "Just female intuition," she said.

"I'm proud to be your partner," said Mattheus, "and proud to know you."

His words felt like honey pouring through Cindy's veins. They warmed her and gave her strength and energy. But even though she was glad to have solved the case, even though Kendra was being released from jail that very day, Cindy still felt deeply saddened by the outcome. Margot had lost both her husband and son, and the thought of Nell bearing the burden for the sins of her family made Cindy ill.

"It's not totally fair," said Cindy. "Nell was just over eighteen, so she'll be charged as an adult and accomplice."

"Nothing's totally fair," said Mattheus. "This kind of victory is often bittersweet."

"More bitter than sweet," said Cindy. "I grew to like Nell very much. I'd say she's more of a victim than a criminal."

"The courts will take that into account," Mattheus said.

Cindy wondered. "Maybe," she said. "What does it say about the sins of the father resting on their children's heads?"

Mattheus grimaced. "You did the best that you could do. This is not work for the faint-hearted." He put his arm around her for comfort. "You have to face that you did an amazing job."

"I saved Kendra's life," Cindy said, "and destroyed her daughter's. A quirk of fate."

"And now we've got to move on," said Mattheus. "There are a lot of calls that have come in about new cases. One in particular, I think, will interest you. It's on St. Bart's." Mattheus grimaced, looking out. "This one strikes close to home."

Cindy wondered what he meant by that. As she studied his pained expression, she wondered if this victim had been killed in a similar way to his former wife.

Cindy felt overwhelmed at the idea of jumping onto another case. She didn't know if she had the strength to go on, the strength to look deeper into murders. And most of all, the strength to grow closer to Mattheus.

She sighed as she looked out at the horizon, at the devastation left by the storm. She knew she had another tough decision to make. She felt Clint's presence with her strongly, urging her to accept, to find vindication for him. As she saw the sun break through a patch of dark clouds, she thought that maybe, just maybe, she'd say yes.

DEATH BY DESIRE
Book #4 in the Caribbean Murder Series

In the midst of gorgeous St. Bart's, a few days before Christmas, a senator's daughter is found stabbed and strangled on the beach—the day after her engagement party. While the rich and famous are pouring in to celebrate the holidays, the local police are desperate to keep it quiet and not cause an uproar. But the senator's family wants justice for their daughter, and they hire Cindy and Mattheus to solve the crime.

As Cindy and Mattheus investigate, they meet the elite crowd surrounding the senator's family, an exclusive world of unimaginable wealth, of luxurious parties on yachts and private villas. They learn of all the people who may have wanted the young woman dead, all the jealousies and rivalries, the secret exes and affairs. They meet her devastated fiancé, her twin sister, and her distraught mom—all intent on the killer being found. They meet the corrupt police force, who wants them stopped, and a rich Russian mogul who controls half the island—and has his own agenda to bring down the senator.

As they delve deeper, they learn the many secrets of this exclusive family and the young woman, and discover that all was not as perfect as it appeared to be. As they get close to the answers, Cindy faces personal danger, while at the same time her relationship with Mattheus grows deeper—and faces a crisis of its own.

And as the two of them are about to leave the island, a sudden twist in events changes everything. Ultimately, they come to learn that on the pristine, perfect St. Bart's, everything is not always as it seems to be.

DEATH BY DESIRE is both a stand-alone novel and Book #4 in the Caribbean Murder series, following DEATH BY HONEYMOON (Book #1), DEATH BY DIVORCE (Book #2) and DEATH BY MARRIAGE (Book #3). Books #5 – #8 in the series are now also available!

Books by Jaden Skye

THE CARIBBEAN MURDER SERIES
DEATH BY HONEYMOON (Book #1)
DEATH BY DIVORCE (Book #2)
DEATH BY MARRIAGE (Book #3)
DEATH BY DESIRE (Book #4)
DEATH BY DECEIT (Book #5)
DEATH BY JEALOUSY (Book #6)
DEATH BY PROPOSAL (Book #7)
DEATH BY OBSESSION (Book #8)
DEATH BY DEVOTION (Book #9)
DEATH BY BETRAYAL (Book #10)
DEATH BY REQUEST (Book #11)
DEATH BY ENGAGEMENT (Book #12)
DEATH BY SEDUCTION (Book #13)
DEATH BY TEMPTATION (Book #14)
DEATH BY INVITATION (BOOK #15)

THE TOM'S RIVER SAGA
A PERFECT STRANGER (Book #1)

THE KILLING GAME
INVITATION TO DIE (Book #1)

Printed in Great Britain
by Amazon